I0788224

Forbidden & Taboo Erotic Sex Stories:

Erotica For Adults- First Time Lesbian, MILFs, BDSM, Bi-Sexual Threesomes, Hot Wives, Anal, Dirty Talk, Spanking (Orgasmic Collection)

Written By:

G.G. Goode

Goode Publications

Table of Contents

Story 1 - Mother Lover (MILF) 3

Story 2 - Rosy Cheeks (Spanking) 32

Story 3 - The Best of Both Worlds (Bisexual threesomes) 53

Story 4 - Filthy Mouth (Dirty Talk) 77

Story 5 - Cherry Chapstick Lips (First time lesbian) 103

Story 6 - Love Me Hard, Love Me Better, Love Me Dirty (Hot Wives, Anal and BDSM) 134

Story 7 - Elevator High (Forbidden Fantasies) 173

Story 1 - Mother Lover (MILF)

Weddings were annoyingly tacky and bound to amount to nothing in the end. That was what Connor had always believed since he was eight years old. Few marriages survived these days and even fewer still lasted more than a decade—just like his parents' marriage hadn't. It wasn't like divorcing was in any way easy business, either. Everyone knew how messy it could be.

So why was it that so many people still went for the idea of marriage when even he could tell that they weren't going to make it? Was he the only one who could, or did no one have the balls to tell them? Or worse, simply didn't want to hurt their feelings? Connor was pretty sure divorce hurt everyone more. Did they choose to turn a blind eye and see everything through rose-tinted glasses instead?

Connor didn't understand. He could see it clear as day when two people wouldn't make it. Usually.

But these two... yes, these two were special. These two were different. They would succeed; Connor was sure of it. The love Rick and Jill shared was unlike anything he'd ever seen before. Genuine. Unconditional. Soul-transcending. It was so strong that Rick and Jill were sure to spend the rest of their lives together—no question about it.

It didn't matter that they were only twenty years old. They were one of the rare lucky couples meant to represent the true institution of marriage. It was intended for people like them.

Maybe it runs in the family, Connor mused, smiling as Rick and Jill kissed, sealing their married titles. The crowd erupted into cheers and whistles, clapping as the newlyweds began their descent down the gorgeous gazebo. Connor caught Rick's eyes and grinned, nodding his acknowledgment. Rick's eyes twinkled in return, their gleam so bright that Connor knew he had never before been happier.

Soon enough, their gazes broke; Rick continued to silently greet his guests and accept their congratulatory shouts, tightly holding hands with his young new wife. Jill did the same, grinning just as widely as he was.

When they were past Connor, his stare thoughtlessly went somewhere else. It followed the crowd and sought out the front rows, settling on a dark-haired middle-aged beauty hugging her husband's arms. Her eyes were full of unshed tears, ready to spill at any moment. Connor's heart skipped a beat.

Mrs. Harris was always a sight to behold. Any day at any time, she was a walking angel, blinding those around her with her grace. Her elegance. But today... Today, Mrs. Harris was something else entirely. Today, she was a vision of happiness; a perfect picture of breath-taking motherly pride.

Though every woman tended to be a mess when their son was getting married, Mrs. Harris was the best of them all. Connor had never before felt so strongly a parent's love of their child. But Mrs. Harris was portraying exactly that.

Somehow, that made Connor happier for his friend than watching him and his bride walk down the aisle.

He and Rick were good friends. Not close enough to warrant Connor a spot as one of his groomsmen, but Connor didn't mind. Even if they had lived together for the past two years—along with three other guys. Their schedules simply never matched up enough in those two years, so naturally, they never got many opportunities to get to know each other better.

Connor frankly wished that they had. If solely for selfish purposes: he could have seen Mrs. Harris more often. The most Connor had seen of her was at their apartment; at times, she would come over to bring Rick a few home-cooked meals—which she also always made big enough for all of them to share—but that was as far as their interactions had ever gone, really. It was a damn shame.

It still didn't stop her from entering his fantasies, however. A lot. As in a *lot*, a lot. It was a secret Connor made sure never to slip up on—Lord knows how Rick would react. Maybe he wouldn't be mad, but Connor was pretty sure no child ever wanted to hear their parent was the subject of their friend's dirty, dirty fantasies. No matter how hot the parent was.

Besides, it was already fucked up enough that Connor was picturing her covered in his cum when Mrs. Harris was such a happily married woman. Not that there was anything inherently wrong with that—but having witnessed first-hand the strong and genuine love that Mr. and Mrs. Harris shared, it was hard for him not to feel guilty about tainting the image of their perfect romance.

Especially when Mr. Harris was so nice and kind. And big. Connor was pretty sure the man could destroy him in a single punch.

But fucking hell, imagining Mrs. Harris on her knees in front of him, sucking him off with all her guaranteed expertise never failed to make Connor cum like a brazen Olympian masturbator—and that was only *one* of his many favored imaginations for every time he came to fap-town. And he went there *often*.

Not that he was obsessed with it. At least, he was pretty sure he wasn't.

As the crowd shuffled inside the nearby hotel lobby for the wedding reception, Connor lost sight of Mrs. Harris and knew it would be too obvious to try and relocate her. He followed the horde of wedding guests, straightening his shoulders as soon as they hunched, then noticed two of his and Rick's other roommates assembling with the bridal couple under a fairy light canopy. It seemed most of the guests were there in order to take pictures.

Connor smiled as many began to join in and photobomb and briefly considered jumping in on the fun, too, but he refrained. There would be time for pictures later when it was less busy. Going right now seemed like it would be a little crazy.

"Connor," someone greeted him.

Connor stiffened, his cheeks blooming red as he whipped around with embarrassing speed. He knew that voice. He'd recognize it anywhere—never needed more than a breath to realize who it was.

"Ah—Mrs. Harris."

Her answering smile was bright. Connor somehow managed to blush even further. He cursed himself in his head.

Only Mrs. Harris ever made him blush. He hated it. Anyone who knew him would immediately be suspicious of what was going on between them.

But she was way too lovely and kind for him to even begin thinking about holding it against her. It was impossible.

"I'm surprised you weren't up there with Aaron and Dmitry," she said. Her lips were so vibrantly red. Delectable. Connor wanted to taste them.

Bet they'd look even better on my coc—

Blushing further, Connor forced himself to snap out of the train of thought before it got anywhere too flustering.

"Oh. Yeah, I mean—Rick and I aren't—" He clammed up. *Aren't what? Close?* It would seem rude of him to say if he was at Rick's wedding in the first place.

Connor cleared his throat and rubbed the back of his neck. "We didn't spend as much time together as he did with them. Those three were always together. But Rick and I… You know. Work and all that." Offering her a small smile, he hoped that none of it would come off the wrong way. He was pretty sure it wouldn't, but one could never know. He had a record of unintentionally stepping on people's toes in his past.

Mrs. Harris smiled wider, and she put her hand up briefly, as if to halt the argument. She shook her head. Connor's shoulders sagged in relief. "Oh, I think it's just because he felt compelled to let Jill's brother be his third groomsman. He probably would have picked you otherwise."

Connor smiled back. Mrs. Harris was always so kind. He was sure she meant it, too, even if Connor was pretty sure that Rick still wouldn't have picked him. He was still closer to other guys. "Thanks. Congratulations, by the way. You must be so happy. I know your family is really close to Jill's. They grew up together, right?"

Mrs. Harris grinned. "Rick and Jill were practically in love since they could walk. You could never keep those two apart."

"Sounds like them alright." Connor's smile widened and he shook his head, thinking back of every moment he'd been a witness to their relationship. They were absolutely over the moon for each other; two soulmates lucky enough to have found one another. Early on, too. Who even met the love of their life back when they were in diapers anymore?

"And how is your family?" Mrs. Harris prodded, tilting her head in genuine interest. It made her look adorable. Not that she ever wasn't.

His eyes dipped to her red, delicious lips again. He swallowed and quickly met her gaze once more. "Oh… They're fine. Thank you. Just as boring as ever. Mom's been bragging about me to all her friends, though, so that's been amusing."

"Oh? What did you do?"

"Nothing," Connor said, his smile returning. "I'm just the first to graduate college in our family. With honors on top of that." His chest filled with pride, and he squared his shoulders. It still felt so good remembering the way his mom cried the day he got his Bachelor's in Health Sciences. "I'll be starting my Masters in PT in September."

Mrs. Harris gasped, and she clasped her hands in front of her mouth. Connor grinned in the same moment a squeal tumbled out of her. His neck turned bright red as Mrs. Harris threw her arms around his shoulders and crushed him with a hug.

"Connor! That's so wonderful!" she gushed, squeezing him tighter. For a moment, Connor thought he even felt her lips brushing against his ear, but he couldn't be sure.

It was probably his imagination. Right? There was no way Mrs. Harris was flirting with him right now.

So into his thoughts, he didn't even realize he never took his chance to hug her back before she already pulled away from him. His brain screamed a thousand curses at him, and it left Connor a little lost because wasn't it his fault in the first place?

"So distracted," Mrs. Harris said, her voice having never sounded so soft. Connor even dared to say she was *teasing*.

Mrs. Harris patted his cheek then carefully traced the line of his jaw. Connor's head clouded over entirely. Was he going crazy? This couldn't be happening. It couldn't. Could it?

"Come on, then," she whispered, her lips quivering up at one side. Her eyes gleamed with mischief. "Why don't you follow me, and I'll give you your graduating gift."

Holy shit. Holy *shit*. It was happening—He wasn't going crazy. Mrs. Harris was actually seducing him!

Connor's jaw slackened until his mouth actually dropped. Mrs. Harris grinned. She didn't waste a moment taking his wrist in her small hand. She started tugging him along down past the fairy light canopy and open bar where so many were gathered, shooting a shudder up his spine. His stomach tumbled when she threw him a hot, inviting look over her shoulder, heart thundering like a wild storm as they quietly slipped into the hotel lobby.

Connor couldn't think. Too stunned by the fact this was actually happening and very similar to some of his many wet dreams, too panicked about being caught and capture Mr. Harris' full enraged attention because he obviously loved his wife very much. It wasn't even fully about how the man could easily pummel him to death. Mr. Harris had always been so kind to both Connor and everyone around him. He was a loving father and adoring husband—the prospect of being the other guy to someone like him was simply appalling. Whoever tempted the wife of such a wonderful man surely had to be the lowest scum of the earth.

His thoughts must be showing on his face, Connor realized, because when Mrs. Harris next glanced at him over her shoulder with her mischievous eyes, the gleam in them faded with her surprise. Her smile waned and her thin brows rose. In the next breath, everything melted with sympathy.

"Don't worry. Fred knows," she said. Her smile was gentler. "We're in a… Hm. What do they call it now?" She put a finger to her lips and looked up pensively. "An open relationship? Polyamory? I'm not sure. Fred and I always knew these types of things as consensual non-monogamy. We've never thought we'd want to try it out. But we're both very happy with the freedom it has given us." She smiled, tugging more insistently on his hand. "I'll tell him about it tonight. He already gave me permission to sleep with anyone I wanted at the wedding. So don't feel bad."

Her gaze trailed over Connor, its burning desire igniting a fire in his bones as it went. Connor's guilt vanished. His breath caught in his lungs as Mrs. Harris sharply pulled him aside to a more secluded hall as they neared one. Her hand ran up his chest, warm even through his dress shirt—the touch so heightened by Connor's lack of his other senses that it sent a shiver up his spine.

Mrs. Harris giggled, seemingly able to feel it. She fisted both hands in his jacket and tugged him towards her in the darkness, their noses touching. "I've seen the way you look at me, Connor... It feels good to be this wanted by someone who is not my husband. Don't you want to have a good time together?"

A blush flared at the back of Connor's neck. His mouth dried, and his heart pounded. Silently, he nodded. He couldn't find the words to say anything as she led him further down the hall into a room, he was pretty sure was staff-only. It seemed to be some kind of storage closet of some sort, but he didn't have the time to inspect and confirm his guess as Mrs. Harris slanted her lips over his and rendered his brain to complete putty.

He was hard within an embarrassingly short time. All Connor wanted to do was touch her—anywhere, everywhere. So he did; slipping his hands over her silky dress to caress every curve of her body, take in every inch of softness she had to offer. It was downright nirvana.

In the past, Connor never understood why it was that he liked older women so much—but maybe it was because of this. Their confidence, the amazing plushness of most of their bodies. Mothers, especially, were particularly wonderful. With fuller hips, thicker thighs—and bigger breasts, too. All probably from the labors of birthing and nursing a child.

Not that Connor tried to think about that much. The last thing he wanted was to actually date a mother and become appointed their child's pseudo-dad. He wasn't anywhere near ready for *that*.

But fuck did he love fucking mothers. They were always less preoccupied about the imperfections of their bodies—the opposite to the many insecure girls Connor slept with through college. Connor loved that. There was something so sexy in the way they didn't squirm at half his touches, and how they didn't ever avert their gazes when his face was buried between their thighs.

And Caroline—Mrs. Harris—was already the very best of them all. There was nothing but encouragement from her. From the moment his hands found the perfection that was her ass, she was all delighted sighs and sweet moans. Cheeky grins and approving murmurs. She never even flinched as he roamed his hands over the thickness of her thighs, instead she leaned further into him, copping feels of her own.

When she expertly started undoing the buttons of his dress shirt and pushed his suit jacket off, Connor's heart skipped a few beats. It continued to do acrobatics as she smiled up at him, besotting him even more with every second. Mrs. Harris was a vision in all her gorgeous glory. And she was with him. Right now. Intending to have sex.

Holy shit.

"Is it just me or are you still all up in your head?" Mrs. Harris teased, smoothing her warm hands over his now-bared chest. Her eyes crinkled up at the corners.

Connor felt like he could barely swallow at all. "Still processing that this is actually happening, to be honest." He silently cursed himself for sounding so pathetic.

But at least Mrs. Harris found it charming. With a giggle, she grinned and gently pushed him back—just enough to be able to reach a hand out at the back of her dress. Connor heard a zip and instantly felt like his brain short-circuited. The next thing he knew, her dress was pooled around her feet...

And Caroline Harris stood in front of him, completely bare except for her pretty lace panties.

Connor's mouth dropped. He stared unblinkingly, void of any thought.

"Like what you see?" she prodded, her adorable smile shifting into a devious smirk. She tugged him forward, her sweet little hands guiding his hands on her body. One of them unabashedly presented him with her breast, nipple already peaked to perfection. Holy fucking *balls*, her tits were amazing.

Connor brushed his thumb over the dark nipple and Mrs. Harris hummed, arching into his hand. He wasn't prepared for the way she grinned at him after, or for her to grab his tie so assertively. He felt like prey—in the best way.

"Be a good boy and take off your pants, won't you?" she whispered.

Connor's control snapped. Mouth thinning, he aggressively pushed Mrs. Harris against the wall and slanted his lips on hers in a possessive, passionate kiss. Mrs. Harris had no complaints. Instead, as he started undoing his pants, her small fingers enthusiastically joined him in his task. Connor let his dress pants drop to his feet before proceeding to cup her jaw to angle her for a deeper kiss. It wasn't long before he hauled her up around his hips by her plush, round ass and instinctively grabbed for her breast again greedily.

His mouth soon followed the same path, leaving her reddened lips to make its way down with wet, sloppy kisses. The sound his sweet Mrs. Harris made when his lips closed around her nipple was so damn good it tore a groan out of him. He wanted to hear it again. Now.

Determined, he rolled his tongue over the stiff peak and ended with a hard suck, pride puffing out his chest as Caroline's breath hitched in return. Her fingers dove into his hair, raking through his locks. She hummed, then tried to tug him even closer.

"You sure are good with your tongue, Connor…" she murmured, scratching her nails across his scalp. It almost had him shuddering.

What was successful was her compliment, though. It was enough to have fire roaring in his veins, teeth-gritting with desire. He needed to give her more, give her something to *truly* merit the praise and—

A strangled laugh left his mouth, and Connor growled just as he dropped to his knees, quickly flipping Mrs. Harris around. He sank his teeth into one ass cheek far before she even had the chance to gasp, dick twitching in anticipation as her musky scent invaded his senses. He briefly glanced up to find Mrs. Harris leaning her forehead against her arms, those of which were now folded against the wall.

The sight had his mouth drier than a California summer.

Pulling away, Connor made quick work of her lacy thong and licked his lips, earning himself a breathless laugh. He frowned. Intent on killing off that sound, he spread her cheeks and dove straight for her rosy folds. Her laugh died instantly, replaced instead by a surprised moan. Connor groaned. He didn't waste time getting to work, slowly sucking and lapping at her nether lips while he reached one hand further up between her thighs.

Mrs. Harris was quick to catch on. Panting, she led him exactly where she needed him, whimpering approving sounds as he began to handle her clit with quick, firm strokes. His dick twitched again, begging for attention. He'd never been so hard before—so hard it physically ached him.

Fuck, he could cum just like this. Eating her out and hearing her moan, feeling her shift her thighs to open wider just for him. Most of the girls he'd been with had been embarrassed and self-conscious when he went down on them, which took out a lot of the fun—but not her. Not Caroline Harris. She was so fucking perfect.

Before long, Mrs. Harris started quivering, her panting breaking off into shorter staccatos of heat and pleasure. It surprised him; though Connor didn't have a porn star's equivalence in experience, he still possessed enough to know without any doubt what such tell-tales meant. Especially when his prime focus in any of his sexual encounters had always been trying to get his partner off—only it was hard to pull off the first time with basically anyone.

And yet here Caroline Harris was, ready to go off like a rocket any second now. With little more than brief guidance on her part.

Christ, that meant she was definitely having a *really* nice time with him. Because it sure as shit wasn't for his skills. He was good—but he wasn't *that* good.

Not enough to get her off this quickly anyway.

"Connor," she gasped, her voice hitching on a moan. Her hand reached back blindly to tangle in his hair. Her hold was a little rough, but fortunately, Connor liked it. He liked it even more when she pulled on his short, curly locks again, drawing a pleasure-pain hiss out of him. If he could speak, he probably would have asked her to do it again. Mrs. Harris whimpered. "Connor, get up. Please. I don't want to cum with your mouth on me. I want to cum around your cock. Now."

Holy fucking Christ on a cracker. She definitely didn't need to tell him twice.

Pulling himself up to his feet, Connor kicked his dress pants away and raced to push off his underwear, nearly making a fool of himself in the process as he tripped over them. Luckily, he managed to catch himself in time and Mrs. Harris didn't seem to notice his mishap—or at least, didn't seem to care enough to acknowledge it. His face sweltered red from both the embarrassment and his feverish desire, though it leaned more towards the latter as his gaze set back on Mrs. Harris' sweet cunt. He bit back a groan, unable to help himself from giving his cock a few solid pumps.

That Mrs. Harris noticed. She giggled and had his gaze shooting up at the sound, unprepared for the mischievousness swimming in her pretty eyes as she stared at him over her shoulder. The look was both seductive as it was devilish; Connor swallowed against his suddenly dry throat, hand still around his aching cock.

Mrs. Harris settled her palms flat on the wall before widening her legs and slipping a hand between them, her ensuing moan enough to make any teenage boy promptly cum in his pants. Connor was sure he would have if he'd heard it many years ago. The best porn couldn't even compare to the beauty of that sound. His brain melted so badly that he could barely process anything else.

"Are you even listening to me at all? Or does this wet pussy just take all your senses away? God, look at you. You're so hard just looking at me. I wonder how you'll feel inside me. Don't you wonder, too?"

Connor blinked and looked up at Mrs. Harris, the words leaving her mouth finally registering once more. He blushed harder and sought to distract them both by running both hands over her perfect ass.

It didn't work.

"Well hi there, welcome back," she murmured, giggling softly. "You sure know how to make a woman feel desirable, I'll tell you that..."

The fingers rubbing her clit moved down, sliding along her wet folds with a bite to her lip. She was tempting him—daring him to fill her. She smiled, gazing at him with what he could only call a challenge.

"Connor. Come here," she whispered, reaching back to spread herself for him. Connor's breath stopped. "I think I know a much better place to put that cock of yours in... Somewhere that'll make us both feel better."

Sweet Jesus' ballsack. Connor's thoughts slipped away from him, pre-cum dribbling from his slit as he stared at what her fingers presented him, wet and ready. He made some kind of strangled noise, both hands snatching out for her deliciously thick thighs. He wrapped his fingers around himself once more, holding his cock steady as he rubbed against the soaking wet cleft of her legs.

He didn't expect Mrs. Harris to reach down between them and position him at her opening, the move so hot and unforeseen that Connor swore it took him everything not to lose it and cum right there.

Shaking, he thanked every God out there for giving him the control. His heart pounded against his rib cage, mind spinning in a whirlwind of bliss as he began to push himself inside. He braced himself against the wall, eyes closing and a moan slipping from his parted mouth.

Until an epiphany struck him.

"Wait," he choked out, retreating and running a hand over his face. He gritted his teeth. "Fuck. Condom?"

Mrs. Harris looked back with another tempting smile, her gaze the perfect picture of seduction. She opened herself up again with one hand, wiggling her ass in invitation. "If you're clean, it's all good. I'm clean, too. And I've had my tubes tied a long time ago. So you can cum inside me as much as you like, honey."

The devilish smile she sent him right then burned away Connor's last thread of self-restraint. His chest rumbled with a guttural noise somewhere between a growl and a moan, bringing out an absolutely feral side of him that Connor never even knew he had. He positioned his cock at her entrance and this time, wasted no breath at all slipping inside her depths.

Mrs. Harris gasped, hips dipping towards him to take in more of what he had to offer. Connor bit his tongue, thrusting shallowly to coax her body to open up to him some more and squeezing her thighs so tight he was sure she would find them bruised later. They both moaned when his hips met her ass and a series of colorful swears danced on his tongue.

"Fuck, you make me want to cum already," he hissed, licking his lips. "You feel so good, Mrs. Harris."

"Caroline. Please—Call me Caroline," she replied, whimpering. She reached down to touch between them where they were joined, mouth parting with a soft moan. "Fuck me, Connor," she said. "Cum inside me. I know you want to. I know you've been dreaming about it. So fuck me until you do. Please."

Connor snarled and promptly heeded to her demands. Maintaining his death grip on her thighs, he started slowly thrusting and rolling his hips at first to test the waters of how wet and hot she was before steadily increasing his pace and the force of his movements. Soon, he was fucking her like a madman, bracing one hand against the wall to better leverage himself while she cried out and both uttered encouragements and praise.

It was unlike anything he ever imagined; feeling her squeeze around his cock, hearing the sweet sounds falling from her mouth, watching the way her ass rippled with his every thrust—it was a piece of fucking heaven. He wanted to be there every day, to never have to stop. And God, hearing the way his name fell from her lips... It had never sounded so good on anyone else. No other girl had made him feel like this, no other girl had ever riled him up so much he could barely hold himself back. Only Mrs. Harris—no, no. *Caroline.*

"Caroline," he panted, moving her in time with his thrusts, eyes squeezing shut at the blinding bliss coursing through him.

Caroline answered with a moan, rolling her hips into his on his next thrust, sending them both into a grinding mess desperately seeking friction. He groaned and bent down to rake his teeth over her neck, relishing the way her fingers slipped through his hair. He hoped she'd pull on it again—like she had earlier. Fuck, he really hoped she would.

"Just like that," she encouraged, her breaths choppy and hot. She ground back against him again and moaned, tugging at his locks to pull him even closer. Connor sucked in a breath, growling and grinding right back into her. Christ, her pussy felt so good. So, fucking good. "*Yes.* God, you're so good. Such a good boy. Such a great *cock.*"

A feral sound slipped from his throat. Connor sank his teeth into the tender flesh of her neck, seeing white. Shit, he was going to cum if she kept talking like that. He wouldn't be able to keep up—to make her fall apart, too. And there was no way he could let that happen now. Not when he'd been dreaming about having Caroline Harris like this for years. Not when she'd haunted his nights with seductive promises and mind-blowing orgasms that left his briefs a mess and left his sheets sweaty.

Every. Single. Time.

He couldn't let her down now that he finally, *finally* had her at his mercy.

But then Caroline squeezed her muscles down on him so deliciously that his knees nearly gave out and Connor's eyes snapped wide open, hips stuttering in their rhythm.

This was it. His end was finally here. He could see it so clearly, just within reach. His thrusts turned from steady and rough to wild and frantic, desperate for release. His balls tightened. Caroline's pussy kept closing around him. Connor moaned freely, teetering on the edge. He swore under his breath, eyes slamming shut yet again.

"Fuck. *Fuck.* I'm so sorry, Caroline, I'm gonna—I'm gonna cum," he gasped. "You feel too good…"

God fucking damnit. He wouldn't be able to get her there. He wouldn't get to fulfill his dreams, and she'd be too disappointed to give him another chance. How laughable was it that on the brink of his greatest orgasm ever, Connor could feel like such a royal fucking failure? He wanted to cry. He wanted to moan. He wanted to cum so hard it hurt. He wanted to make *her* cum twice as bad.

But then Caroline turned to look at him over her shoulder and smiled, her cheeks so gorgeously flushed, and she slipped a hand between her legs. Her smile vanished, face twisted in bliss as she gasped and moaned instead. The sight sent Connor spiraling into bliss, brain exploding into nirvana as he spread her ass cheeks wide and ground out his milky release inside her, moaning unabashedly.

He was so loud he was sure someone had to have heard them, but he didn't care anymore. Not when he was having an orgasm this good. Not when he was with the actual woman of his dreams, spurting his cum deep inside her. Nothing else mattered.

He was still riding out the last waves when Caroline joined his high, crying out and milking every last drop from him with her sweet cunt as she ground out her release. Connor gasped and bit his tongue, groaning gravelly as he fought to keep them both upright. His knees shook, his breath stayed caught in his lungs, eyes wide.

Holy. Fucking. Shit. That was… He couldn't even manage to find the words. Fantastic? No. That couldn't even begin to describe what had just happened between them. *Jesus. Best sex of my fucking life.*

The only regret he had was that he hadn't gotten to actually watch her cum. He'd been in the throes of his own orgasm, too busy having his brain explode via his dick to be aware of anything else than how good he felt in the moment. It was a damn shame he couldn't hold out for her.

Still, the utterly sated smile on Caroline's lips was mostly enough to make up for it. So was her undeniable contentment, conveyed clearly in the way she sifted her fingers through his sweaty hair and hummed, sighing like she didn't have a care in the world.

"Did I leave you speechless?" she teased, when neither of them had spoken for a while.

How long had it been? Five minutes? Ten minutes? Less? The concept of time seemed so silly and inconsequential right now.

Caroline wiggled against him and giggled, the move pushing out his slowly softening dick. Connor swore he caught a pout before she turned her head away from him and bent down to pick her panties up. She slipped them on and went back down for her dress as well, beginning to make herself presentable again.

When she noticed him staring, dumbfounded, she grinned and offered him a wink. "You know, for someone still so young, you're definitely sprightly," she said, pulling out a hand mirror and wipe from her clutch. She moved on to fixing her make-up with such ease it was evident she had often fixed any post-sex smudges before.

Connor's heart did funny things in his chest. A blush rose from the back of his neck to the tips of his ears, intense in its heat. It was all frankly a little dizzying.

It must have been noticeable, because Caroline blinked and huffed the most adorable little laugh. She shook her head. "Keep that up and you'll have a bright future in your sex life. You'll make a lot of women happy."

"I don't think I can take all the credit. I almost didn't make you cum. You had to help yourself along, remember?" Connor didn't even know how he managed to string so many words together. Currently, his brain still felt like it was putty. Like he wouldn't even be able to count to ten. But his words were true, however.

Caroline smiled and patted his cheek. She shook her head and shrugged. "Sex is never entirely all about someone else's experience. I've learned a lot in almost thirty years. And as a mother of two. Mainly that no partner should leave the other to do all the work. You have to help each other out. Especially when it comes to orgasms."

She winked at him again, here, and Connor flushed even deeper. Jesus, it was ridiculous how much this woman could make him blush. Caroline thumbed the redness of his cheeks and grinned, her gaze briefly dipping down at his limp length. She licked her lips, and Connor swore he would have stirred to life again if his body didn't need time to recharge, still.

Jesus. Mrs. Harris was so fucking hot.

And tight, he mused with twitching lips, remembering the way her hot, wet walls clamped around him. Whoever said women who had given birth became loose and dry were deluded liars of enormous proportions. Caroline Harris was pure proof that they would be just as good as any other woman. Maybe even better. They could still be sexy as hell, even at forty or fifty years of age.

He must have looked deep in thought because the next thing he knew, Caroline laughed and called his name, seemingly amused or maybe even slightly confused. He blinked and shifted his attention on her once more, heart thudding loudly at her bright smile.

"Connor…? Hey, are you listening?"

In an instant, her smile was gone. Connor blinked and tilted his head, washed over with a sense of confusion.

The sudden change was a little too odd, a little too abrupt. "Yeah? What is it?"

But Caroline's stare remained unchanged, unwavering. Her expression captured the same steadied level of confusion and... something else. Concern? But why?

"Connor!"

A hand waved in front of his face and Connor startled, jumping a little as he suddenly found himself back on the lawn near the fairy lights canopy, where so many were still huddling in order to snap some pictures with the bride and groom. Mrs. Harris was standing in front of him, brows knitted together and sporting a faint frown.

She'd been the one to wave her hand in front of his face.

Oh, God fucking damnit. Had it all just been a fucking fantasy?

"Connor, are you okay?" she asked, much like any worried parent would to their child.

So unbelievably sweet. So caring. So beautiful. Jesus Christ, she was so perfect. Of course he had to be daydreaming. There was no way in hell he could ever land a chance with her. Especially not with her husband in the picture.

Unless they would really have an open relationship—but they've never seemed the type. I don't think either of them like the idea of sharing each other.

His heart deflated in his chest, whizzing like a punctured balloon. Even if Mr. and Mrs. Harris *did* have an open relationship, Connor suspected she probably wouldn't be interested in guys around her son's age, anyway.

Damnit. His throat worked up a swallow. "Uh… Yeah. Sorry. I got a little… lost there. Caught up in some thoughts."

It wasn't exactly the whole truth, but at least it wasn't an outright lie. He couldn't very well tell Mrs. Harris that he'd been fantasizing just now about fucking her in a hotel storage closet. Especially when they'd barely spoken much before today.

Can't exactly bail and say it was a joke, either. I doubt she'd find that funny from an acquaintance—one of her son's friends, no less.

Thankfully. Mrs. Harris didn't press for more details. She merely nodded, concerned features giving way to relief.

"Oh. Good." She smiled; amiable but strictly platonic. His heart continued to deflate miserably. "Well, like I was saying… Your parents must have thrown quite a celebration for your success. I know I would if ever Rick graduates with honors, too. Fred would probably splurge the most. I wouldn't be surprised if he'd decide to surprise us overnight with cruise tickets." She chuckled fondly, shaking her head. "Now I have no other choice but to push him harder! We haven't had a family vacation in too long!"

Connor huffed. *As if there's a chance in hell that Rick wouldn't get honors,* he thought. But apparently Mrs. Harris misinterpreted his reaction, because she frowned deeply in return. His chest began to pound in a staccato of panic.

"Are you kidding? Rick is at least twice as smart as I am. He's the genius one out of our little circle. Always has been. You've got nothing to worry about—he's a wonder child. No doubt about it."

Mrs. Harris' eyes widened, then she laughed—the sound so melodious it took Connor right back to his fantasy. He had to shake the thoughts from his head so as not to lose himself from the moment again. But at least he could take some comfort in the fact he would never get her beautiful laugh wrong.

"Well," she said, sweeping her long dark hair back over her shoulder. "That's what you get when you get two brainiacs and put them together."

She grinned proudly, and the delight was so blinding that Connor couldn't help smiling back, even with all of his growing disappointment towards reality. Caroline Harris would never want him, and Connor would never know what it felt like to be with her, inside her. To hear her truly moaning his name. He'd never know what her wet cunt felt like—even what it tasted like.

"What's going on? What are you two so smiley about?" someone called from his right, happy and bemused.

Connor glanced at the newcomer to find Mr. Harris, faintly smiling and eyes crinkling as they always were. Especially when he was looking at his wife. Which he was, right now. Of course Connor couldn't blame him.

Mrs. Harris smiled at her husband, too, reaching to take his hand in hers. "Connor graduated with honors, honey. Isn't that wonderful? We were just talking about how proud you and I would be if Rick graduated with honors, too."

"You graduated with honors? Connor, that's great! Congratulations!" Mr. Harris clapped Connor's back and grinned, shaking his shoulder like all proud dads did. It reached something deep within Connor—though they barely knew each other, Mr. Harris was always so warm that he never came across as anything but genuine. As such, none of his compliments ever rang empty.

He's a good man. Good husband. Good father. He and Mrs. Harris are lucky to have each other.

Mr. Harris said something then, something about excusing him and his wife as they needed to get going— Jill's parents had been looking for them both in order to take official wedding pictures. Or something like that anyway. Connor had been too caught up in his thoughts.

As they walked away, he ran his hand through his hair— that of which was still perfectly coiffed and missing the wildness that fantasy-Caroline-Harris had made a mess of.

Jesus Christ, I'm so pathetic. Fantasizing while the hottest mother in the world was talking to me. Typical.

At least he'd been lucky enough not to soil his pants. He didn't know how he hadn't actually cum. Maybe because he hadn't been sleeping. But that fantasy-orgasm was definitely the best one he'd had yet—even counting the real ones.

So at least there was that.

Story 2 - Rosy Cheeks (Spanking)

This was probably the worst idea they'd ever had.

Any minute now, Dominic's parents could come home from the grocery store. Could walk in on the pair of them moaning up their house in a heated frenzy, their trip having panned short for the day. Dom found it terribly unlikely, but it wasn't exactly reassuring. For all they knew, maybe his parents would make a quick detour home after Mr. Reavers forgot his wallet again, in which case they might have even gotten caught already...

Still, Rosie couldn't bring herself to care. Not when Dominic was making her feel this good. This dizzy in the best way there was. Especially when they never had many chances to be like this in the first place. Not when Dom lived five hours away.

Stupid dream-colleges.

Dominic grunted. Digging his fingers into her hips, he leaned his weight on one elbow and rolled his hips against her ass in a slow circle, driving a shudder up her spine. Rosie whimpered, eyes squeezed shut tightly. She bit her lip as Dom mouthed the back of her neck, tasting the sweaty skin there.

Palming her side with his free hand, Dom groaned and rolled his hips harder. "Christ. You feel so good, Rosie," he whispered, burying his face in her hair. He resumed rocking, building up to his previous steady pace and sending her toes curling. Bracing himself against both the bed and her hip, he made sure each thrust buried him as deeply as he could go, as deeply as her body would allow him. Rosie gasped and spread her thighs wider, cheeks flushing hotly. She needed more.

Dom groaned, the hand at her hip running up her side again. A slow smile spread over his lips, which Rosie only knew was there because she'd felt it come to life against her shoulder. "God, I missed you. I missed the way you feel around me. I missed knowing how much you love having me inside you."

Flustered, Rosie's blush grew more feverish. She hid her face in his bedsheets, fingers curled around them for dear life. While Rosie had always cringed when Dom's talk got a little dirty in the bedroom, she still hadn't mustered up the courage to admit it to him despite the fact they'd been dating for the past six months. And despite the fact they'd actually known each other their whole lives. Dom was her first—everything about sex was still embarrassing to her. Though she *had* gotten a little better at not being so self-conscious of her naked body, lately...

It was hard to care when Dom was so clear about how much it always turned him on.

"You're so wet," he murmured, propping himself up from his elbow so he could palm her ass with his free hand. Humming, he grabbed one full cheek and held on to it possessively, picking up his pace until he settled into a beat of rough little pounds. A small cry left her lips and was promptly muffled against the sheets. Rosie moaned, spiraling in a mess of bliss.

"Oh God," she gasped, arching her back and trying her best to meet his thrusts. The grip she had on his sheets was death-like and her eyes remained clenched shut tightly. Rosie swore she could still feel his stare, though. Settled in the space where their bodies met, watching the way his cock pounded into her.

Dom always liked doing that.

Slowing down his pace, Dom sighed and ran his hand up from her ass to her side, then finally around to one of her full, peaked breasts. Rosie bit her lip when he played carefully with her nipple, recalling how different his touch was from three months ago when they'd only started getting sexual. He'd been too rough, back then—not from any lack of experience, but simply because none of any of the girls he'd been with had ever been as sensitive as Rosie. And it wasn't exactly like she had been much help letting him know as much, either; as her first real boyfriend and sexual partner at the tender age of twenty-two, she hadn't known much about herself in that department.

Even now, Rosie still wasn't used to how good Dom was when it came to sex. Jesus, he was good. *So* good. More than that, she was still trying to get used to how embarrassing some things were about sex. Awkward bodily noises, squelching bodies, communicating what humiliating things felt good—those were all part of a slow progress to accepting these things were normal.

She was just too shy. Too stuck on her innocent image, as Dom once said. There was nothing shameful about what they were doing or how good he was making her feel—no matter how differently her church-going parents might think.

Rosie was so glad to have Dom. He was a good partner—a good lover. She wasn't even sure sex would have been this good and comfortable if it wasn't for him. Even if they had his level of experience. Dom was a kind man—one who always sought to make sure she was comfortable with whatever they were doing. One who always went out of his way to make sure she liked what he was doing and who always sought to learn what she liked best—all for the sake of making her cum.

Jesus, he was good at making her cum.

She just wished they could do this more often than every few weeks. He left her wanting more each and every time.

Dom's hand left her breast. Peppering wet kisses over her shoulder, he halted his slow rocking for a moment to seemingly shift in a new position, yet Rosie was still helpless against stopping her whimpers from slipping out. She was barely aware of the soft, "Sorry baby, give me a second," that Dom murmured with a kiss to her lower back before both his hands found her hips again and pulled her snuggly against his lap, fully seating himself within again. Rosie let out another muffled cry, instinctively grinding back into him for some friction.

There was a beat of silence and then Dom chuckled warmly. He ran his hands from her hips to her ass, rubbing both cheeks with such heat and want, that it had her burning up from the inside. "Did that feel good, Rosie? Much better than a vibrator, huh?"

Her flushed cheeks returned with a vengeance and she buried her face deeper in his sheets, swallowing. "Dom… Stop it. You know I don't have one…" she whispered.

"You should," he replied, resuming moving and slowly building up a rhythm of steady, firm thrusts. He grunted and grabbed her hip in one hand, steadying her as he found a beat that pleased them both. "Then you'd miss having my cock inside you even more. Miss *me* more."

Rosie whimpered, her grip tightening around the sheets. She wanted to tell him how much she already missed him all the time, how much she touched herself thinking about him, but she couldn't. She met his thrusts eagerly instead, mouth parting as one of his hands slipped around and beneath her belly to play with her clit. She bit down on the blue fabric and cried out, fingers squeezing down on the soft sheets until all her knuckles were surely white.

God, his experience was so obvious in times like these. As his girlfriend, Rosie knew she should probably feel jealous towards the fact he so clearly knew his way around a woman's body—but she couldn't make herself care when it meant he could so easily draw out pleasure from hers.

"Dominic…" she moaned, begging him silently. She needed more, she could see her orgasm in the distance, getting closer and closer. She met his thrusts with more vigor, gripping his bedsheets even tighter.

A hand landed on her ass, swift and nearly painless. Rosie gasped, eyes snapping open wide as her pussy clamped down on him. Dom kept moving, grunting out his pleasure. He didn't seem to have caught on how much she'd liked the slap. He never seemed to notice anytime he smacked her ass and Rosie wanted to let him in on it—wanted him to do it more. Do it harder.

But she couldn't. She was too embarrassed to admit it. She only knew Dom spanked her on an instinctive level, loving the way her ass jiggled in return.

Dom's hand fell on her ass again, a little harder this time. Rosie gasped and whimpered, automatically bucking back against his cock and grinding. Dom groaned, thrusting harder. Faster. Rosie started trembling, breaths erratic as her mind spun out in bliss. Her path to orgasm was getting clearer, closer, steadily more inevitable with every—

Dominic smacked her ass again, and Rosie's eyes snapped open wide. A raw cry tumbled from her mouth, the pain stinging her so good this time that it sent her crumbling apart instantly. Distantly, she thought she might have heard Dom swear but Rosie was too caught up in the waves of her orgasm, too busy trembling like a leaf and grinding out her high against his cock that she couldn't be sure. She was pretty confident that Dom was helping her draw out each wave, though, vaguely aware of hips rolling back into hers and incoherent murmurs floating in the room.

And her stinging ass cheek. A delicious pain that only added to the glow of her release. One that she wanted to experience again and again. Every damn day they were like this.

God, she would love that.

Only when Rosie was coming down from her high did she become aware of Dominic lovingly kissing her shoulders and the back of her neck. The embarrassment rushed through her instantly, flushing her body head to toe with a dizzying blush. Jesus Christ. She'd just orgasmed the second he spanked her harder than usual. When she was close, but needed more effort, more friction. More *something*. She couldn't believe that all her buildup had ultimately been outgunned by a simple, rough slap to her ass.

Did that make her a pervert? Oh my *God*.

If she was lucky, Dominic wouldn't know any of that though. He'd have to take credit for making her cum—which he had—but he didn't have to catch on to all the details, right? Right?

God, Rosie hoped she was right. She couldn't bear the thought of Dom knowing she was so… so… *so damn far from the innocent girl he grew up with*.

"Fuck, Rosie… I missed feeling you cum. Squeezing all around me like that. And how you sound…" Dominic buried his face in her neck, sighing with complete contentment. He smiled against her skin and kissed her nape lovingly. "I was surprised, though. I knew you were close. I could feel it. The way your body was all tensed up and how you kept clamping down on me. Trembling and grinding against my cock like that. But… I didn't know you were *that* close. Hm? What's up with that, Rosie?"

Shit. Oh God, he totally knew. He totally knew that something was up and that it hadn't just been his usual skills. Damnit. *God freaking dammit.*

Silent, Rosie kept her face buried in the sheets, too flustered to even acknowledge the comment. She swallowed, fighting against her furious blush to at least try and not look so guilty of being coaxed to sudden orgasm by something so embarrassing.

Dominic chuckled and kissed her nape again, mouthing a path of slow, sweet kisses down her spine. Then he flattened himself against her back and buried his face into her neck once more. She couldn't help her gasp as the change nestled his cock deeper inside her, sending her squirming. Dom's lips quirked up against her skin in a clear grin, one that had her heart skipping a beat.

"You know… I notice that you seem to tense up and moan every time I spank your ass. I wasn't sure about it before, but I'm pretty positive that I'm right after today. You weren't there yet. I could feel that. Close, but you needed more to be able to cum. And I know you didn't just cum because I was fucking you good. Or because it's been three weeks since we last had sex. I spanked you hard and you instantly fell apart beneath me. That can't be a coincidence, can it Rosie?"

Rosie's throat worked in another swallow. Something about the way he was asking her was so sexy that it made her blood feel as though it had turned into hot lava. Her pussy throbbed, something had Dom's grin growing. Her face burned so hotly she grew dizzy.

Still, she didn't reply—she couldn't. She was completely mortified. What would people say if they knew she liked pain in the bedroom, however little? God, what would *Granny* say? Could she even look at her in the eye upon going home tonight?

Dominic's chuckle reverberated against her throat and he scraped his teeth against the skin there in a mock bite. Rosie shuddered, biting her lip as he left a trail of slow, wet kisses all the way up to her ear. He nipped the small lobe.

"What, did I leave you speechless, Rosie? Should I do it again just to confirm my suspicions?" he asked, tone dripping with equal amounts of teasing as it did temptation.

Rosie gripped his bedsheets tighter, swallowing down a moan of misery. She wanted to die. God, she was so embarrassed. And Dom knew it, but he still pushed her further, tried to get her to admit it. Or maybe even make fun of her.

Reaching for the closest pillow, Rosie whacked Dominic in the face as best and as hard as she could, quickly grabbing another to hide it in. Dominic laughed. She pouted. She clutched the pillow closer, whining. "Stop trying to embarrass me. You're being mean."

"I don't need to try," Dom gibed, grinning as he kissed her shoulder. He shifted off her back, presumably straightening himself up, then ran his hands over her sides, down her thighs, and over her plump ass. She glanced back just in time to see him licking his lips as he stared at the space they were joined. He slowly started moving again, setting up a languid pace. "You're already embarrassed."

Rosie went to protest, but Dominic's hand flew punishingly against her ass, tearing a moan from her lips. She clasped her hand over her mouth, her furious blush returning with a vengeance. Dom grinned, so cheekily proud that she needed to look away. She buried herself back in his pillow, praying his parents were still ways away from coming home because at this rate, Dom would have her moans ringing throughout their house.

"My oh my… You really *do* like it," Dom teased, running his hand up her back.

Rosie whimpered. Reaching back, she grabbed his arm, holding onto him firmly while he picked up his pace to something more patterned and rougher. It had both their breaths breaking into heavy staccatos of pleasure.

But then Dom chuckled, leaning down to kiss her wrist before pulling away from her grasp—seconds before spanking her ass again. Rosie muffled her moan into the pillow, evermore mortified by how much she loved it— though her back still arched and shuddered like a traitor to her own mind. Her pussy was, too.

"You're so impossible…" she mumbled, mind fogging more and more as she tried her best to match his thrusts. She could barely manage, though; even after a few months of sporadic but very enthusiastic and intense sex, it was hard to be able to keep up with him when Dom made her feel so damn good.

Dominic laughed affectionately and leaned down to kiss the back of her neck, all sweetness and silent love. He melded himself against her back so they could be close once again then braced himself against the bed with his elbow, thrusting harder. Rosie gasped and whimpered, attempting to muffle her moan in her pillow. Dom groaned and tugged it away before she properly could though, needing to hear her.

"You should be telling me these things, Rosie. I would have done it more often before if I knew. What else do you like, hm? What else have you been holding back from me all this time?"

I like when your cock is inside me. When you hold me down and fuck me, Rosie thought. Her cheeks flushed redder than the ripest tomato. God, she could never tell him that. She couldn't handle him knowing how dirty her mind could get. Not when she'd always been a little innocent Rosie, daughter of his mom's best friend and virgin until twenty-two years of age.

So she said nothing and stretched out a hand to his hip instead. She moaned and Dom swore under his breath, slipping a hand over her side and chest. He palmed her breast, taking care to remain gentle even in his fervor, and nipped her ear. His chest rumbled with a strange mix of a growl and a groan.

"What... nothing? You don't like me trying to figure out what gets you off? You don't want me to make you cum?"

Rosie smacked him firmly, frowning. She panted and dug her nails into his skin, loving the way he hissed. "Don't be ridiculous, Dom," she mumbled.

Dom chuckled and tugged on her lobe with his teeth, then pulled back to sit up on his knees like he had been moments before. Rosie's heart stuttered, knowing what was coming. He was going to fuck her good and proper, just like he had earlier.

Yet the words that left his mouth in the next breath told her he had other immediate plans. "So you won't mind if I do it again, will you? Heads up."

Rosie's eyes widened and her mouth dropped. She turned to look at him over her shoulder, face burning. "Wait, wha—"

Dominic's hand cracked across her ass and Rosie flinched, her elbows buckling underneath her weight. She bit back a heated moan, eyes squeezing shut and fingers twisting in his messy, sweaty blue sheets. Dom groaned his approval.

"Fuck. Yeah, you definitely like it..." he murmured, tenderly rubbing the sore cheek he just abused. "I can feel it. I can feel you squeezing around me. Like you're trying to milk me dry..."

Rosie barely had the time to process how hot his words were before he spanked her again, even harder than he just had. Her breath caught and a cry left her lips, her hips bucking instinctively against his cock. He cursed as she ground her ass on him, needing more.

He slammed his hand across her ass again, his chest rumbling. "God, I missed you, Rosie. You feel so fucking good." Another slap. Rosie gasped, eyes rolling at the back of her head. Stroking the sore ass cheek, he murmured, "Tell me if I do it too hard, okay?"

Rosie barely had the sense to nod, but she did. She knew she had to—he wouldn't go on without her explicit permission. If those past few months of sex had taught her anything, it was definitely that. Whether that was simply because that was how he had always been or if perhaps her lack of experience made him more careful, she didn't know. Maybe it was even a mix of both.

Dom delivered another slap then, and Rosie's mind promptly went blank. She whimpered and arched her back, biting her lip when he started picking up his pace. So badly, she wanted to push herself up on her hands to better meet his thrusts, but Rosie couldn't. She couldn't manage; her arms were trembling too bad, too weak from her recent orgasm and the onslaught of bliss coursing through her.

Slap. Her walls clamped down on him, a strangled moan spilling from her mouth. *Slap.* She gasped, her walls quivering around his cock. *Hard slap.* Rosie winced and whimpered. Her sore cheek throbbed in protest—but she loved it. Loved how much it hurt. It was the best pain she'd ever felt, the only pain she wanted again and again. God, why hadn't she told him earlier that she liked this so much?

"Rosie," Dominic panted. His voice was strained and full of bliss. "Rosie, I'm gonna cum. But I want you to cum too, baby. What—" He groaned. Slowed his pace to something languid, squeezing one tender ass cheek. "Tell me what you need. I know you're close... I can feel it. Tell me what you need, Rosie."

Rosie moaned, too flustered and full of bliss to be able to respond. God, he was so good. She was so close, needing just a little more. But then his hands wandered all over her back and sides, feverish and needier than they'd ever been—coaxing her—and Rosie whimpered, realizing his pace wasn't going to change until she let him. Until she told him what she needed.

She knew she couldn't cum at this rate.

Letting her desperation for release overwhelm her, Rosie whimpered and pushed herself up as much as she could manage. Trembling, she caught one of his wandering hands and guided it down between her legs, hoping with all her might that Dominic would understand. He did— barely even a breath later. She whimpered when he started stroking, just the way she liked.

Dom groaned gruffly and started moving faster, harder. He kept working her sensitive button, bracing himself with a single hand on her ass. Rosie moaned loudly, using all her energy to keep herself upright. She wanted to rock back into him and meet his rough thrusts, but she was too weak, too zapped of strength to be able to manage. Dom didn't seem to mind, though, not once relenting his frenzied pace.

"Again?" he asked within a groan, his voice so incredibly strained.

Rosie could only frantically nod, moaning with abandon. She didn't care anymore whether or not his parents were home and could hear her. All she wanted was to cum. Touching herself by her lonesome never felt this good, this fulfilling. God, Dom was so good. So, so good. Only he could make her feel like this. Only he could ever let her innocent walls down. Only he could ever make her cum this hard and—

His hand left her clit to harshly smack across her ass and Rosie flinched, the most feverish moan spilling from her mouth. She crumbled in bliss, trembling like a leaf as she gripped his sweaty bedsheets like a lifeline, chanting Dom's name like a mantra. Dom followed closely after her, spilling himself inside with a series of curses and incoherent syllables.

At least, she was pretty sure they were incoherent. It was hard to tell when her brain wasn't exactly working right, at the moment.

As they both came down from their highs, Rosie lazily smiled as Dom bent down to plant soft, wet kisses along her back and shoulders, tenderly rubbing the abused ass cheeks. Now that the rush of sex was fading, Rosie was distinctly aware of how sensitive the skin was—and how even such a gentle touch was almost too much. Still, she let him; after all, since they'd had such an intense session, Rosie knew that there was no way Dom would even dare handle her roughly.

Dom pulled back and he sighed in pure, undeniable contentment. Rosie expected him to roll over on his side, finally spent. Instead, she startled when lips brushed her tender, aching flesh—causing her to blush all the way to her roots.

She gasped.

Before she could think of anything to say, though, Dom chuckled warmly and teased, "Rosie, your cheeks are all... *rosy.*"

Eyes widening, Rosie erupted into bits of loud laughter, those of which were intense enough that she quickly struggled to gasp in breaths and soon felt her ribs start hurting. Jesus, Dom was so ridiculous. So, so ridiculous. A complete goofball and silly monkey.

But God, she loved him for it.

Rolling over on her back, Rosie spread her arms for him and continued to giggle as he obliged and hugged her, slanting his lips over hers. He kissed her deeply for a while, feeling up her side and cupping one breast tenderly. She shuddered as he played with her nipple, a sigh escaping her mouth. Dom smiled and rolled them over, so she lay on top of him; blissed-out, spent, and a little sore.

They stayed like that for a while, touching each other lovingly and sharing slow, lazy kisses.

"Think your parents are home?" Rosie murmured, her cheeks reddening. "Because I might need you to hide me forever if that's the case. I don't think I can look at either of them for the rest of my life knowing that they heard us…" She cleared her throat and buried her face in his neck, hiding herself. "Well… Heard *me*."

Dom puffed a laugh, the sound reverberating against her lips. It made her heart do all these funny things. Sometimes—usually in moments like now—Rosie dearly wished either of them would have admitted their feelings for each other a long time ago. They wouldn't have been pining for so long, wouldn't have been deprived of time and moments like these before he had to move out of town.

Then again, maybe it was best that they had so many years apart. Both of them had still been discovering who they were and what they liked, and Dom had always said that he learned so much about women in college. For all she knew, maybe Dom wouldn't have been such a wonderful lover and boyfriend if he never got to learn from those women.

Hm… No use dwelling on what-ifs now, she thought.

Dom turned to kiss the top of her head, smiling still. "Nah. Told you—Mom likes to go through every alley. We won't be seeing them back anytime soon. Plus, I think Dad wanted to stop by the hardware store after. Wants to replace some tools or whatever."

He attempted a shrug, but it was hard with Rosie lying on top of him, which made her smile. She kissed the line of his jaw and cuddled him closer, pleasantly exhausted and utterly satisfied. God, she missed moments like these. More than the sex, she missed the intimacy they shared afterward; missed the slow touches and sweet, drawn-out kisses. She missed being so... connected to him. Emotionally. Physically.

She wondered how he'd react if she suggested moving in together soon. She was still saving up money for college—maybe she could look into going to his. Or would that be too clingy? She just wished they didn't have to wait weeks to see each other. Wished she could wake up to his sweet, gorgeous face.

Familiar hands cupped her ass a little too enthusiastically and Rosie instantly winced and exhaled a sound of discomfort, one eye squeezing shut tight. Okay, so maybe he had spanked her a little too hard. Now the pain was too much to be pleasurable. Or was that normal as the glow of sex waned?

Fortunately, Dom seemed to notice that she was no longer comfortable.

"Shit. Sorry, I didn't mean to—Hang on, I'll go get you something."

Dom kissed her temple and gently let her slide to the mattress. Swiftly, he pushed himself off the bed and tugged on his briefs and pajama pants before hurrying out of his room and down the hall. Rosie held her breath and squeezed her eyes shut, begging every God out there that she wouldn't hear his parents. She sighed in relief when she only heard Dom rummaging around.

It was a few minutes before Dom came trotting back, holding a glass of water in one and in the other… a pack of frozen peas?

"Uh… What are those for?"

Dom offered her a cheeky smile, the one he so often gave when he would awkwardly scratch the back of his head—only his hands were full. He shrugged. "I couldn't find where they kept the cold compresses."

A second of stunned silence passed, and then another. Rosie's lips twitched and she started cracking up hard. "Dom! Seriously? Oh my God!" She continued to laugh and shook her head. God, her boyfriend was so silly. She loved him so much. "Put those back. I'm not putting frozen peas on my butt, thank you very much. Your parents are going to eat those someday."

"But—"

"Just bring me some gentle oil or something. Or cooling lotion. Anything that…" Her cheeks flushed, and she averted her gaze shyly. Rosie cleared her throat. "Anything that, you know… speeds up healing."

Silence was all that met her in return. Confused, Rosie's gaze flickered to Dom's once more to gauge his reaction, finding him smiling at her with awe. But there was something more to his expression. Something she couldn't quite pinpoint. Like amusement or a newly unveiled epiphany, or maybe—

Mischievousness, Rosie realized. Her face flushed. Whatever Dom was about to say next, she was pretty sure she wasn't going to like it.

"You read up on it," he said, his tone full of wonderment and playfulness. It wasn't a question.

Rosie blushed harder and groaned, grabbing a pillow to hide her face behind it. "N-No! I—I did not! It just happened to be on my dash. I was just—I was curious! I didn't do any research of my own!"

She peeked over her pillow to see Dom grinning in that way she so loved, and her heart skipped a beat. Had she not felt so flustered, she probably would have smiled back.

"Well, we should," he said, handing her the glass of water. She accepted it quietly. He sat at the edge of the bed, putting away her pillow and brushing a lock of hair away from her face. "Is this something you'd like to bring into our sex life… fairly regularly? Because I loved spanking you. And I loved how much *you* loved it."

Rosie bit the inside of her cheek and took a long sip of water, fighting hard against her blush trying to creep up all the way to her ears. Honestly, with how much Dom turned her into a tomato, she was surprised her face hadn't accommodated to being flushed all the time.

Still, she met his gaze shyly and nodded, covering his hand with her own. "...Yeah. That'd be nice. I'd like that."

Dom's eyes twinkled and his grin spread wider. He leaned in for a few quick pecks then pushed himself to his feet once more. He pointed behind him. "Awesome. I'll go get my laptop, too, then."

Rosie gaped. "What—Right now?! I didn't mean right *now*!"

Laughing, Dominic slipped out of his room, racing down the hall as he had earlier. "I did!"

Groaning, Rosie flopped on his bed and hid under his sweaty bedsheets. She buried her face in them, her blush forever present on her cheeks judging by the way they still burned. Still, she smiled thinking about how excited Dom was. All because he wanted to find out more about what she liked, start honing more skills to ensure he could make her cum.

Because Dominic was in love with her. Loved her just as much as she loved him. Would do anything for her, just as she'd do anything for him. No matter how embarrassing.

Snuggling up inside his warm sheets, Rosie sighed. She could only hope his parents wouldn't pick up on the fact that the two of them had been playing hooky while they were gone.

Story 3 - The Best of Both Worlds (Bisexual threesomes)

If anyone asked her, Sophie was sure that they wouldn't believe her if she said that Ezekiel was resistant to the idea of having a threesome with her and another girl. Because that was what men always dreamed about, right? Fucking two girls and getting to watch them kiss and fondle each other all in the same night. What guy in their right mind could refuse that?

But it *was* true, though. After Sophie had suggested the idea post-sex one night, he seemed into it. At first. But whether it was because of his mind-blowing orgasm or sleepiness, it was laughable how quickly he seemed to change his mind. How weary and not quite sold on it all he became. He would question her relentlessly, make sure she wasn't only wanting this for his sake. That made her laugh even more. Since when had she done anything sexual only for his sake? That's what she'd reminded him.

He was uncomfortable. That much was clear. But Ezekiel tried to play it cool, tried to shrug it off like he was just being the generous one who was only looking out for her. He wouldn't even take the out anytime she offered it to him. Probably because he was stubborn.

"You know, you don't have to do this. I can find someone else. Or just wait some other time. Whenever the

opportunity presents itself—it's fine! Just don't feel pressured, Zeke."

"What? No. I want to," he'd argued, affronted. But his eyes were already shifty.

Sophie rolled her eyes.

Maybe Zeke was nervous that he wouldn't be able to perform. Or maybe he was just terrified that it would change the bond between them steeped in friendship and lust. They were best friends with benefits—there had to be a limit to what they could do before shit got complicated or something, right?

But he came through in the end, however hesitantly.

"Are you sure about this?"

"You're asking me if I'm sure? You're the guy who's about to sleep with two women at the same time. And get to watch them touch each other and make out. Shouldn't I be the one all antsy?" She laughed.

Of course, no one could ever know any of that now—not with the way Zeke was reacting. Sophie had never seen him like this. With such little composure and wild eyes, such hunger and fire in his touches. He was no longer too anxious or in his head. In fact, he probably wasn't even thinking at all—his mind too full of desire and wanton pleasure as he watched. Waited. Caressed.

"Oh, you're a lot of fun," Katarina murmured, sliding up Ezekiel's body with slow, wet kisses.

It was comical how much Zeke was turned on. His pupils were blown, blazing like tiny embers, his breaths so heavy and choppy you'd think he was having a panic attack. Sophie bit her lip to keep from laughing.

Katarina grinned once she'd made her way to his jaw, nipping along the line of it teasingly before pulling back to draw Zeke in a long, hot kiss. Zeke groaned, squeezing her waist.

Katarina smirked, pulling on his bottom lip. "Most guys I've been with have been so prissy when they didn't get any attention for long. They had other ideas in their head, you know? They wanted two women all over them. Didn't want to feel left out."

Zeke's chest rumbled but he didn't comment. Sophie suspected his brain still couldn't process much beyond the fact there were two naked women in bed with him. He dragged Katarina in his lap properly, winding his fingers into her long brown hair. Sophie's lips twitched as she watched, imagining the hands she was roaming over her body were his. *Theirs*.

"Some even thought they'd get to dictate everything that us girls should do. Wanted us to follow their every command," Katarina went on, chuckling. "That didn't sit too well with me. Because you see, I've always liked women better. If you gave me a choice, I'd choose to fuck women over men every single time. They're so much better... so much more attentive. So much more invested in every way. Wouldn't you agree?"

Zeke groaned in what could have been a yes or a no—or even an 'I don't care'. Katarina smiled. Sophie bit her lip and slipped her hand past her belly, curling against the aching wetness there. Slowly, she started to thumb her clit, sighing as the waves of pleasure lazily rolled over her. The sound instantly drew Katarina's attention; she peered back at Sophie, lips curling wider to form a grin. She coaxed Zeke to look at her, grabbing his chin.

"See? Sophie here only has to watch me kiss you and talk to you about how much I like women before she has to touch herself. Makes me wonder what she'd do if I'd touch you... Which we *can* find out. Because you don't mind when a woman's in charge. You don't mind whatever the fuck we do right now—something tells me you'd be happy just watching me finger-fucking her all night. But I'm not that mean... Don't you worry."

Sophie's breath caught as she watched Katarina's hand dip down between their bodies, feeling along Ezekiel's chest and his abdomen before curling around his cock. Zeke cursed and shuddered with a groan before she even started jerking him off, the image a strange mix of hilarious and hot. Sophie smiled and pulled her hand away from herself to crawl over to them, wanting in on the action.

Zeke was the first to take notice. As soon as Sophie was within reach, he broke from Katarina's kiss to grab her wrist, catching her lips with his. Sophie moaned. God, Zeke had always been such a good kisser. She never learned where he'd picked that up but whoever had taught him was a good teacher. The things he could do with his tongue… With one messy, passionate kiss, he could easily leave her wanting, throbbing, begging to be filled.

This kiss was no different.

The one Katarina dragged her into was somehow even better, though—maybe because her hand kept working Zeke's stiff cock, pulling tricks that had Zeke grunting and cursing. Sophie shuddered when she even managed to make Zeke moan, a string of vivid curses escaping him just before he muttered something like, "Christ, this is so fucking hot."

Sophie wholeheartedly agreed. Moaning in the kiss, she ran her palms over Katarina's breasts and circled her fingers around Katarina's dark nipples. She pinched both of them.

Katarina grabbed hold of her bottom lip with her teeth, a half-moan spilling from her throat. "God, I love girls."

"Shit. Me too, babe," Zeke concurred roughly, surging forward to close his mouth around one of Katarina's peaked nipples. Katarina inadvertently freed his cock and sighed, burying a hand in his unkempt hair to pull him closer.

Sophie laughed. She agreed with her own hum before dipping one hand between Katarina's legs. She started playing her cunt as she would play herself, pulling Katarina in another slow, heated kiss.

Katarina's breath hitched. She pulled away and tossed her head back, mouth parting with a soft, "Oh…"

Zeke let out another string of colorful curses, nipping her nipple before manhandling Katarina in his lap so she could better face Sophie instead. Sophie smirked, pride swelling inside her chest. Zeke smiled back, all mischievous eyes and devilish intentions. Katarina seemed to notice their exchange, smiling back at her and pushing her hand closer against her wet cunt.

Sophie's heart skipped a beat, pussy throbbing in response. God, being with a woman was so amazing. While she spent most of her life chasing after men and being ashamed of her attraction towards women, Sophie would always remember how liberated she first felt when she finally accepted and understood her sexuality for what it was—and allowed herself to act on her once-shameful feelings.

Being with a woman was nothing like being with a man. Their hands were nimbler, more experienced, kisses patient, more sensual. They knew how to handle women's bodies more accurately than any man could, aware of secrets most men could only learn with time—and sometimes even never would.

Katarina was reminding her of all of that, right now. How different she was from Zeke, how her reactions contrasted with a man's. There was no fighting with herself to sound manly and strong—no fear that her femininity would diminish in their eyes merely for being vocal. She was all shameless moans and beautiful, blissed-out smiles; all slow, burning kisses, and even hotter touches.

Fuck, Sophie loved women. And men. *Both*. She was totally one hundred percent—no, no, one *thousand* percent bisexual. Definitely. Truly, if tonight was showing her anything, it was how good she had it on that front.

She had the best of both worlds. Dick and pussy. An assertive mouth and a sensual one. A partner that could fuck her so good she could barely walk the next day, and another that could make her knees wobbly with only a single, very involved kiss and who never had to search for her most sensitive spots.

God, *damn* Sophie was lucky.

Katarina seemed to think so, too. She tipped her head back again and threw an arm around Zeke, smiling. "Mmm. Right there, baby," she whispered, closing her eyes. She opened her thighs wider for better access, moaning when Ezekiel started mouthing wet kisses to her shoulders and neck. Her ensuing moan was even louder when Sophie applied more pressure to her clit. She grinned and puffed a laugh. Fuck... So sexy.

"My God…. Mmmm can always count on a woman to find the sweet spot without any issue, huh?" she said breathlessly, her grin growing. She was so beautiful and radiant, Sophie was sure she easily outshined the sun.

Sophie grinned. She giggled when Zeke growled and bit Katarina's neck; he always could get so feral when he was exceptionally worked-up—which there was absolutely no doubt he was now. Sophie had never seen him like this before, never seen him so lacking in composure and downright frenzied. It was amazing.

Katarina seemed of similar mind, too, because the next thing she did was huff a small laugh and tug him forward for an awkwardly angled kiss. She moaned when Sophie slipped her fingers into her warmth, rocking against her fingers before Sophie even started circling her clit. A low hum fell from her mouth the moment after, pleased when Zeke cupped one of her breasts and wound his other arm around her stomach.

Sophie's breath hitched. In the process of grabbing Katarina's breast, his fingers had accidentally brushed against Sophie's own nipple, sending a shiver down her spine. The sound didn't seem to go unnoticed; breaking away from his and Katarina's kiss, Zeke looked at her with blazing eyes and grabbed the back of her head to slant his mouth over hers, too. Katarina didn't seem to mind, only giggling and turning her attention to Sophie's shoulders, lips tracing a sensual path of kisses.

Sophie moaned, winding her fingers through Katarina's gorgeous curly brown locks. This right here was absolute heaven.

"This is the best threesome I've had so far—and that's saying something," Katarina gibed, which had Sophie smiling into her kiss with Zeke. She started cracking up, and Zeke bit her lip hard as punishment. Sophie bit him back.

Ezekiel groaned. "This is the best sex I've had. Period," he muttered, drawing Sophie into another hot kiss.

Sophie complained and playfully protested the statement with a smack to his shoulder. Katarina laughed.

"Now don't be rude, Ezekiel," Katarina said. "I'm sure Sophie has given you the time of your life before."

Sophie grinned her appreciation. She pressed her thumb harder against Katarina's clit, drawing her in for a kiss as she gasped.

Katarina moaned. "God, yeah… I've never been so sure of anything in my life. I bet she's the best you've ever had."

"Sure you're not talking about me?" Zeke asked gruffly, his voice hoarse with desire. He went back to mouthing kisses on Katarina's neck… Then slipped his hand down with Sophie's, joining her in her task. "Sounds like you might be self-inserting."

Katarina laughed again, the sound a bit more strangled, this time. It was so oddly hot that it drove Sophie up the wall—and Zeke, too, judging by all the biting and growling he started doing. He started circling her clit more aggressively, urging Sophie to pull away and focus entirely on fingering Katarina's pussy.

The whole mood of the room escalated quickly, after that. So intense that Sophie could barely breathe, silence drowned them easily and filled the air with nothing but heat, drooping their eyes as she and Zeke continued to work in tandem on giving Katarina an orgasm. It wasn't long before she did; after only a few minutes of the three of them sharing passionate kisses and wanton touches, she keened a cry and crumbled apart in their arms, both of her own looped around their necks. She was blatantly drunk on pleasure as she came down from her high, proven by her slurred grin.

"Jesus… You're both really something," she murmured as Sophie pulled her fingers out of her sopping wet heat and Zeke retreated as well. Her smile still had yet to cease, though it waned to something softer. Lazier.

Sophie kissed her, dragging her hands up Katarina's sides all the way to the swell of her breasts. Squeezing one, she rubbed Katarina's own wetness over her peaked nipple, loving the way Katarina moaned and deepened the kiss. Zeke wasn't left unaffected either, muttering out another litany of colorful swears that his mother would surely kill him for before mumbling something like, "Jesus, you're both going to give me a heart attack."

Sophie giggled and smoothed that same wet hand down Katarina's side, up Zeke's strong thigh, and over his abdomen. She felt along the hot skin, the faint ridges that defined his abs. His chest rumbled with a deep growl and her hand continued to crawl up to feel his thundering heartbeat, a grin curling her lips.

It was such a thrill to know that Zeke was enjoying himself this much now. Given how reluctantly he came in about it all, nothing pleased her more. He'd probably forgotten all about wanting to get out of this. Whatever doubts he had, whatever it was that held him back—that was all gone now.

Katarina's hands delved into her hair and Sophie hummed, thoughts clouding. She moaned as Katarina deepened the kiss even more, touching her tongue to Sophie's with such exquisite finesse that Sophie's head got all hot and dizzy.

Her hand fell from Zeke's chest, then down into his lap, blindingly searching for his cock. It didn't take her a second more before she found it. She started pumping him the way he liked, goosebumps rising on her flesh as he started to grunt out his pleasure. Katarina kept kissing the life out of her, twining her fingers in Sophie's brown locks and tugging hard enough that the pleasure bordered on pain.

And then it was Katarina's turn to let her hand fall between Sophie's thighs, finding her clit with ease. She didn't waste a moment to start playing with it, her touch so light Sophie was sure she was teasing.

Sophie gasped, letting out a small cry. Her eyes squeezed shut, hand stuttering in their rhythmic beat against Zeke's cock, which had him covering her hand with his. He needed her to keep going.

"I'd finger you, but I haven't clipped my nails in a while," Katarina said, which frankly took a moment for Sophie to even process through all her blissful waves.

In fact, she took such a long moment that even worked-up-Zeke had the time to process the comment before she did.

"The fuck does that have to do with anything?" he mumbled, taking away the hand over her own to palm both of Katarina's breasts. He bit Katarina's shoulder hard enough to leave a mark.

Sophie didn't have a hard time processing that one. She and Katarina both burst into laughter.

"When it comes to lesbian sex? *Everything*," Sophie said, throwing her head back and rocking against Katarina's hand.

"Don't exactly want to finger-fuck somebody with scissors, do you? Same principle," Katarina added, dragging Zeke in a slow kiss.

Sophie opened her eyes when a hand joined her own, wrapping around her fingers as it gripped Ezekiel's cock, and she grinned when she found that it was Katarina's. Together, they started stroking him in rhythmic beats, tearing throaty groans out of Zeke and turning his face a rare, rare shade of scarlet red.

Sophie was amazed. "Zeke! You're blushing? It's so rare to see you blush for anything," she teased, drawing her hand away from his cock to brush the redness over his cheeks. "Wow. You really are so worked up, huh?"

"Shut up, Soph," Zeke bit out, blushing harder.

Katarina laughed, pulling away from their kiss and letting go of his cock, too. She winked when he groaned. "I think it's time you put a condom on that bad boy. Don't you?"

Zeke groaned again—this time, though, without any protest. "Yeah? Yeah, okay." He shifted her off his lap to reach for the condom on the nightstand, running one hand through his hair. "Just give me a second."

"Take two, take three. Take ten or even ninety," Katarina sang, pushing Sophie back on the bed and climbing over her. Sophie shuddered, gasping when Katarina's hand dove right between her legs, wasting no time to aim for her prized jewel. Sophie instantly wrapped her arms around her, shifting her legs open some more. "I've got something to keep me busy."

"Jesus fuck. That's so hot," Zeke choked out in the background. "Am I seriously not dreaming?"

Sophie wanted to giggle—truly, she did—but quicker than she could have ever anticipated, Katarina started working magic with her knowing fingers and rendered Sophie's mind to mush in seconds. Her moans swallowed any other sound she could make. God, Katarina was so right—women never fumbled around when they touched another woman. They knew which spot was the most important—which spot was the most sensitive and full of pleasurable nerves. Which spot would make them lose their minds the fastest.

And that's exactly what Katarina did to her. Made her lose her mind. Worked her clit in tight little circles that maybe weren't exactly the right pressure, but were still too damn good to make her care to correct her. She could definitely still cum at this rate. Jesus, she wasn't even sure who was swearing right now out of the three of them—was it her? Zeke? Were they all cursing?

Who the hell cares, she thought dazedly, writhing like a cat in heat. She ran her hands all over Katarina, focusing more on her perfect breasts as they kissed with abandon. Maybe the kiss was sloppy, too, with Sophie's desperation, but Katarina didn't seem to care.

"That's right," Katarina whispered. "Such a good girl. You're making me all wet just watching you…"

A low sound that could only come from Zeke rumbled through the room. "Need some help dealing with that?" he asked, his voice gruff with desire.

Katarina's fingers stopped moving and Sophie bit her lip to keep from whimpering. She opened her bleary eyes and struggled to become aware of her surroundings, mouth drying when she found Katarina looking over her shoulder and grinning. Katarina beckoned Zeke forward with a finger. "Mm. If you wouldn't mind…"

Zeke laughed and the sound was so strangled and thick with desire that goosebumps rose on Sophie's flesh. Still, the absurdity of the question wasn't at all lost on her and she giggled along even though her body felt like it was on fire. Never in a million years would Zeke refuse to fuck a willing woman in the state that he was in—and yet here Katarina was, asking him like he would be doing *her* a favor?

Absolutely hilarious.

Surging forward, Ezekiel joined them, slipping his hand between Katarina's legs just as Katarina resumed working her magic fingers on Sophie. She and Katarina moaned in tandem, drawing each other in for a hot, wet kiss.

Belatedly, Sophie realized that Zeke was probably too worked up to finger Katarina properly after everything tonight. Touching her right now—he was likely only testing how wet Katarina was, gauging whether or not she was ready to receive him. Just like he always did with Sophie. Once satisfied and confident, he would slip his cock in and set up a delicious rhythm, fuck Katarina good—

But not me. Not this time, Sophie realized, blinking twice. She began growing envious. More than that, Katarina hadn't even gotten her nails clipped either, so she wouldn't get to experience being filled another way. *Damnit.*

Sophie didn't realize the thought had her pouting until Katarina broke away from their kiss, curious as she met Sophie's gaze. She erupted into giggles—the sounds cut short when Zeke pushed himself inside. They both moaned and Sophie's envy grew, simmering like the sullenest green-eyed monster.

But it wasn't left unaddressed for long. "Don't worry, baby. You won't be left wanting," Katarina said, tracing her bottom lip. "You think I didn't prepare to fill the one between us that wouldn't get to have Zeke's cock?"

Sophie's mouth dried, belly burning with want. She just about quivered with anticipation.

In the background, Zeke groaned. He palmed Katarina's ass and hissed, seemingly acquainting himself with her delicious warmth, but refused to move. Sophie wasn't sure why; either he was exercising patience for her sake or he was simply trying to regain his control.

Whichever reason it was, Sophie giggled. She peeked further around Katarina's shoulder—enough to see his face—and asked, "You okay there, bud?"

"Just struggling not to bust a nut," Zeke returned, squinting one eye open and throwing her a feral grin.

Sophie laughed. The sound turned into a hum when Katarina started mouthing kisses on her throat. Katarina took both her hands and pinned them above her head, kissing a path up to her lips before breaking away and reaching further than Sophie's hands for something. Sophie took the opportunity to push up and capture one perfect dark nipple with her mouth, relishing in Katarina's hitched breath.

"Fuck, your pussy feels so good, Katarina," Zeke groaned, which had Sophie smiling. She giggled more, leaning over to glance at him again and find him with his head tossed back, eyes closed as he set up a steady rhythm. His breath was choppy, chest heaving rapidly.

He wasn't the only one feeling good, either. Above her, Katarina moaned lowly, tilting her head down enough that Sophie could see her eyes were shut, too. She opened them a moment later and smiled seductively at Sophie. Mischief reigned in her gaze as she brought down her hand and revealed what she had been reaching for earlier—a realistic, flesh-colored dildo.

Sophie's heart raced. She held her breath in anticipation.

Katarina moaned, eyes closing once more as Zeke started pounding into her. "Yeah, you don't feel so bad yourself," she breathed back to him with soft, high-pitched whines.

They made Sophie so needy that she pushed up to kiss Katarina again, pouring out all her impatience and sexual tensions. "Don't forget me. Please," she begged, grabbing Katarina's hand—more specifically, the one with the dildo.

Katarina moaned a laugh and kissed her harder, scraping her teeth against Sophie's bottom lip. "Wouldn't dream about it, baby," she whispered.

With joined hands, she and Sophie both brought down the toy to Sophie's wet, throbbing core, rubbing it all up with her wetness. Then, they slowly pushed it inside, Katarina catching Sophie's moan with her mouth. Finally, Sophie was filled; her envy was gone.

If what they were doing before was heavenly, it was nothing compared to them fucking and moving in tandem as they did now. They were a euphoric mess of sweat, moans, and groans—not overly loud like most porn portrayed threesomes but infinitely sexier in their relative quietness. Katarina even matched the pace of her dildo with Zeke's thrusts, setting a strangely more intimate, connected vibe to their encounter. One that Sophie absolutely *loved*.

But something was missing, that much was becoming clear. As good as it all felt, as much as she could see her climax in sight and writhed desperately to achieve it— she was also slowly coming to understand that she likely wouldn't get there unless she got a little more. She needed more... *something*. But she didn't know what.

The realization made her hopeless; made her even more frantic to achieve her end. Sophie wanted so badly to be wrong. She bucked up towards the toy between her thighs, clinging fiercely to Katarina. She whimpered, helpless to the pleasure while she left red marks on Katarina's skin—but none of it seemed to change anything. Even when Katarina dropped down and started sucking on her nipples, bringing shudder-inducing waves...

"Soph—Fuck," Zeke said, something like frustration seeped into his tone. Sophie opened her eyes, hoping to be able to distinguish the features of his face and tell what he was thinking, but she couldn't. Everything was too blurry, tears having long welled up in her dark eyes in the face of all the bliss coursing through her.

But at the next words that fell from her best friend's mouth, Sophie's heart skipped a beat.

"Katarina—Sophie's struggling. I can see it—she wants to cum so bad, but she can't get there. Can you go down on her like this?"

Holy shit, yes. Please. Please, Katarina—Yes. I want that—Need that. So much. Please—

Her lips moved in a desperate plea, but Sophie didn't know that until Katarina let out a breathless laugh and traced her lips, murmuring, "Looks like she loves your idea, Ezekiel."

Sophie's heart thundered, her cheeks heating up. Her stomach raced with wild butterflies, thighs quivering when Katarina pulled the toy out of her. Zeke stilled his movements, likely to give Katarina some space to place herself how she needed to. He still slapped her ass just because he could, though, and Katarina briefly bit her lip.

She drew Sophie in for a short, heated kiss before pulling away and clapping her thigh. "Come on, babe. Scootch back. Let me taste your sweet cunt—I'll make you cum so hard you see stars," she said, smirking. She had all the confidence in the world.

Sophie's mouth watered and she scrambled into position as fast as she could. She barely caught the way Zeke groaned, more aware of his short-winded laugh. "Fucking hell. You'll make us both cum if you keep talking like that, Katarina."

Katarina grinned, throwing Zeke a look over her shoulder that made him shake his head. But when Sophie was done settling, she didn't waste time diving down between Sophie's thighs, throwing her legs over her shoulders.

Sophie gasped and instantly grabbed Katarina's hair, trembling with need. Zeke muttered something she didn't have the mind to hear anymore. Her world was lost. She spun out in her storm of bliss and nirvana as she had just moments earlier, shuddering more and more with every passing breath. Her relief built back up, swirling tighter and tighter in her belly like it never waned, edging closer… closer…

Sophie's eyes snapped open. She moaned sharply, twisting her fingers in Katarina's hair. She threw her head back, spots dancing across her vision. "Fu—Gonna cum," she gasped out, whimpering helplessly.

Her world exploded into stars.

Crying out, Sophie held on tighter than she ever had in her life and rode out her high through all its powerful waves. Incoherent words fell upon her ears, but she couldn't focus, couldn't take in anything else than her glorious pleasure and how Katarina's tongue helped her extend her orgasm for all of its worth. *Holy fucking shit it was good.*

There was no question that Katarina knew what she was doing with her mouth—that perhaps she had given Sophie the best oral she'd ever had in her life. It had been so long since she'd cum this hard—even Zeke was never this good.

When Sophie came down from her high, a sated smile spread to her lips, body utterly spent, and tingling everywhere. Gradually, though, Katarina's moans took her out of her daze; moans which, Sophie realized, were quickly escalating in intensity. Katarina was close.

She tilted her head down to catch up on what she'd missed, belly churning as she finally became aware of the sound of wet, slapping skin. Her cheeks flushed as she glanced at Katarina, blissfully close and moaning, and then Zeke, grunting savagely and face tightened up in concentration. Sophie watched as they fucked frenziedly, Katarina crying out praises and encouragements while she stayed wrapped around Sophie's thigh. Zeke started becoming more and more vocal, grunts turning into groans and growls as he teetered closer and closer—

"*Fuck*!" he bit out, growing tense before he ground himself against her ass stiffly, his mouth parting with an angry moan.

There was a flash of disappointment on Katarina's face— but it didn't last more than a brief moment before Zeke growled and scrambled underneath Katarina's thighs to aggressively eat her out.

The sound Katarina made as his mouth met her cunt was so beautiful and sexy that Sophie moaned as well, reaching down to gently thumb her own clit. It was still almost too sensitive to be played with, but Sophie bore through it, the sight simply too much of a turn-on not to. Katarina grabbed Zeke's hair, pulling roughly. She moaned time and time again as she rocked her face against his mouth and rode it unabashedly.

With a final cry of, "Yes!", she succumbed to the throes of her climax and broke apart. She grounded the waves against Zeke's mouth, her moans vibrating directly on Sophie's thigh as her free arm wound tight around her other. She was a trembling, shuddering mess—so much that Zeke growled, proudly spanking her ass.

He didn't relent his oral assault until Katarina slumped, spent, and boneless. She looked absolutely stunning, bearing a grin so sated that Sophie wanted to kiss her for it—only Katarina was too far down to be able to manage. Still, the gentle nipping she did on her thigh and up along her stomach was enough for now. Sophie sifted her hands through her sweaty hair, exhausted, and content.

Zeke joined them in the next breath, sinking by Sophie's side with the most worn-out groan. But on his lips was still that same satisfied grin.

Gently, he nipped Sophie's nipple. He laved it up with his tongue, sucked the peaked tip carefully, then rose up further and captured Sophie's mouth, kissing her deeply, slowly. The affection coaxed a content sigh out of her. She wrapped one arm around his neck, burying a hand in his damp hair.

It wasn't all innocent, though. However sensual and amazing the kiss was, an odd, earthy tang still lingered on his lips—one that Sophie knew had to belong to Katarina. It made her moan.

A slap cracked through the room and Zeke flinched. Sophie erupted into tired giggles; clearly, the slap had come from Katarina—perhaps in revenge for how he slapped her ass moments earlier. She'd wager a guess that she'd more than likely aimed for his cute tush, too.

Sophie and Ezekiel both looked down, finding Katarina grinning at them both, happy and a little drowsy. They grinned back and let out a blissfully content sigh before Zeke buried his face in Sophie's neck. Katarina was apparently perfectly content to stay down between Sophie's legs, one arm curled around her thigh while the other affectionately traced patterns on Zeke's calf.

"I gotta say, Zeke... That was pretty freaking good oral—from a guy," Katarina said, breaking the comfortable silence.

Sophie felt Zeke grin against her breast. He laughed, the sound reverberating against Sophie's chest. She smiled, too.

"Mm. Can't take the credit. Greatest teacher right here," he said, wrapping an arm around Sophie's waist. "This one wanted to make sure I knew how to go down on a woman."

"Thank fucking God. Best decision ever," Katarina concurred, snorting.

It was Sophie's turn to laugh. She sifted her hand through Katarina's hair, her feelings all kinds of mushy right now. It was probably all the post-orgasm oxytocin. "I don't know, guys. You know what would top that right now?"

"What?" Katarina and Zeke chorused.

"Deciding to order us all some pizza."

There was a collective groan of approval and Sophie grinned widely—more than she had all night. Katarina threw her arm up in a victory air pump and Zeke snickered before doing the same. He then proceeded to kiss her shoulder, already starting to doze off.

"Extra-large, please," he mumbled.

"With extra cheese," Katarina piped in.

Sophie laughed again, humming her approval to both suggestions. Her grin stayed on her lips, the purest content sigh spilling from her mouth. Maybe she was exaggerating, but right now it felt like she had never been happier in her life.

Seriously. A hot as fuck threesome and post-sex pizza with two of the hottest people on earth?

Best. Night. Ever.

Story 4 - Filthy Mouth (Dirty Talk)

Seventy-one days. That was how long it had been. Seventy-one freaking days since he and his wife last had sex.

Andy was at his wits' end.

While this wasn't the first time they'd had such a dry spell, the last had been easily excused to their need to adapt their lives to the arrival of their baby boy, Flynn. They had been tired, but blissfully so, too preoccupied with providing for their child to even think about sex. It had been understandable. Predictable. Easy to overlook.

But this dry spell? It was another thing entirely. Andy couldn't understand it. Couldn't excuse it. Couldn't accept that it was happening for the reason that it was. Flynn was five now, energetic as ever but not as demanding and helpless as he was as a newborn. He and Maryssa had adapted to life as parents, experts in finding and making time to have sex to sate their needs. They were almost, if not just as active as they were before Flynn.

This is why Andy found this complete no-sex-interim totally unacceptable. Christ, they were usually so regular! Four days a week, on average—never less than two! How could anyone blame him for getting antsy about not having sex for *seventy-one* days with his insanely hot wife?

But this had to end. He would let it go on no longer. Their ongoing streak for the lack of intimacy would end today. Andy would make sure of it.

He couldn't let their incredibly busy work schedules be an excuse anymore. He would make time to make love to his wife and remind them exactly why they always set aside opportunities for this. Especially with how stressed Maryssa was with the new store launches from her highly successful meal-prepping company.

This was the first time they were opening several branches across the country for better service, quicker shipping times, and an extended reach for customers, and Maryssa was overwhelmed by it all. She had been so anxious every day simply making sure everything was going along smoothly—a mood that persisted when she got home. She was always too tired at the end of the day to do much more than their responsibilities as parents, but Andy knew she needed to let out all her pent-up stress one day or another.

And what better way than with an orgasm?

Preferably, one he would give to her—and not one she'd give herself all alone.

I wonder if she's been touching herself already? Maybe when I was at work doing some overtime? he mused. *Or maybe in her office bathroom... Maybe anytime she was on a break. Maybe Maryssa thought the same thing I did. Maybe she figured she had to let all that stress out somehow...*

The thought had him growing hard already. Fucking hell, he'd definitely been jerking off too much without her. The worst part was that it was never even *that* satisfying without her. He wanted to be inside Maryssa's tight pussy, feel her walls quivering around him as she came. He wanted to taste her sweet cunt, make her whimper his name helplessly like he always did.

Oh, God, damnit. He *really* was getting too hard now. At home, he probably wouldn't mind but as he needed to actually pay attention to the road and get out in roughly five minutes, it wasn't the smartest thing to let himself get a hard-on. It was bad enough to go out and try to hide a boner in public, but then at his wife's workplace, too? That was insane. Inconsiderate. Beyond stupid and risky.

Andy couldn't allow for her image as the CEO to be damaged by his feral lust. He loved Maryssa too much for that.

But behind the closed doors of her office, however...

Andy shook his head, smacking his own cheek. Silently cursing himself for getting so carried away with his thoughts, he focused on the road ahead instead. For anything to happen in the first place, he figured, he first of all had to succeed in getting there without drawing attention to himself. Or else the dry spell would most definitely go on.

Andy couldn't let *that* happen.

So calm down, Jr. Help a brother out. You're not getting any relief if you can't keep your chill.

Talking to his dick. Jesus. How much more desperate could he get?

Andy shook his head, sighing. He should really just focus on getting to Maryssa's building first. *And* picking up some flowers. The latter wasn't something he needed to do but Andy figured it would be a good, innocuous excuse to come see his wife at the office and he'd been feeling like giving her flowers lately, anyway.

Plus, Andy noticed that it always seemed to put Maryssa in a good mood when employees complimented her on the cuteness of their marriage. With him passing by to hand her flowers just because he felt like it, how would this not warrant Maryssa some of those compliments?

Rounding the corner of Maryssa's street, Andy spotted *Jill's Flower Shop* and was pleased to notice that it wasn't busy. He parked directly in front of the shop. For a minute, he remained inside and made sure he was presentable; triple-checking from different angles that his previously stirred friend wasn't making him spring a third leg through his pants, however faint. Once he was confident, Andy stepped out of his car and headed inside.

He didn't dawdle around in the shop. Knowing what he wanted already, he headed straight for the florist counter and requested a bouquet of white lilies (Maryssa's favorite), holding back his wince as the florist fetched the flowers and then summed up his total. He headed back into his car with a huge grin, already imagining Maryssa's awed response.

Once back, Andy put the lilies in the passenger seat then drove on to Maryssa's building just half a minute down the road. He pulled into his usual reserved parking space which Maryssa had secured for him long ago. He grabbed the flowers and swiftly trotted inside the lobby.

Kimmy, the receptionist, was surprised to see him. "Oh, hey Andy!" she greeted, smiling brightly. Kimmy was always so peppy. Her gaze dipped briefly to the lilies and mischievousness crawled amidst her features. She grinned. "Did you get in trouble with the missus last night?"

"Nope," Andy replied, grinning back. "Just felt like dropping by to tell my wife how much I love her. Maybe grab some lunch, too. Has she eaten yet?" Maryssa always ordered out when she didn't have her lunch, which Andy knew she hadn't brought today.

Kimmy shook her head. "Should I order the usual for you two?"

"That'd be great! Thanks, Kimmy!" Andy said. He hurried off towards the elevator. "Better make the most of the time before she gets busy again, right?"

"Maryssa knows how to take a lunch break, Andy."

"Not before she has food, she doesn't!" Andy piped back.

Kimmy laughed. The elevator closed and started riding up. Andy smiled.

It was true that sometimes Maryssa didn't know how to take a break unless she had food accessible at her hands, but today, Andy was going to make sure that her reason to be busy would be for something that had entirely nothing to do with work. With only about twenty-seven minutes free of interruptions as the rest of her staff also embarked on their lunch, Andy intended to make full use of them to be discreet and sate this unresolved sexual tension from the past seventy-one days. She needed it as badly as he did, he was sure.

When the elevator took him to the top floor and *dinged*, Andy's heart began to pound. He made a beeline straight for Maryssa's office, barely having enough sense to smile and greet back staff members as they noticed him. He could only hope he didn't seem rude to any of them he might not have greeted back.

Maryssa was on the phone when he knocked at her door and peeked in. She looked up, her face brightening like the sun at the sight of him, and smiled so happily his heart melted. She beckoned him inside wordlessly, eyes crinkling as they dipped to the bouquet of lilies. But she didn't stop talking on the phone, her gaze drawing back to a bunch of papers on her desk.

Andy closed the door behind him, quietly making his way around her office to shut her blinds, then grabbed the opportunity to transfer the flowers to a vase. She always kept one on the small desk by the door for presumably occasions like these. Making a quick trip to the bathroom to fill the vase with water, he carefully arranged the flowers and waited for her to be done with her conversation. He pretended not to be listening much, though it was hard to ignore.

She was talking with one of the new stores' directors, he was pretty sure.

"Those boxes need to be shipped out on time from now on. I won't tolerate any more lateness on behalf of your lack of hindsight. I hired you because you were spectacular on your last job and your references all said you were always timely, Mr. Korvick. Don't go proving me wrong now. Prove to me that I haven't made a mistake. Okay?" Her frown persisted, brows deeply knitted together until her shoulders relaxed at last. Andy smiled. Good—so her message was understood. She smiled back at him and winked. "Alright. Good. I have faith you will handle this well. Please call me if you need me to send any help. I know you're adjusting still, and I'd hate to come down hard on a man whose wife is expected to give birth any day now." She laughed, all traces of strict CEO Maryssa gone and replaced by genuine friendliness. "Okay. Good day, Mr. Korvick. Take care."

After she hung up, she stretched long and loud, throwing Andy a cheeky smile. When she was done, she stood and crossed the room in quick steps, snaking her arms around his neck. "That was one of our new branch directors. He really thought it was an acceptable excuse to say that he didn't have enough hindsight to hire more packaging staff in order to meet the shipping dates. He was late by two days. Can you believe that?"

"Honey, I don't have the skills to organize *anything* effectively," Andy deadpanned with a grin. He pulled her closer to him by her waist. "Honestly, I would have been twice as late shipping those out—and that's if I really tried! So maybe he's not doing so bad."

"Some people rely on those boxes to eat every day, Andy. They need to be on time," Maryssa said, rolling her eyes. She smiled and leaned in for a quick kiss. "This is why you will never work at my company, by the way. Have I ever told you that?"

"Like, ten thousand times."

"Good. This makes ten thousand and one."

Andy laughed. "I missed you," he murmured, drawing her in for another kiss. It was longer but still just as sweet, lingering on enough that Maryssa hummed a sound that was almost a moan.

She pulled away before he could deepen it, seemingly unaware of his intentions. "Oh, Andy, they're beautiful!" she said, obviously addressing the flowers. She trotted over to them, thumbing the petals of a lily and smelling it. Her smile widened as she turned to look at him, those pretty eyes gleaming so gorgeously. "What did you bring them for?"

Andy's heart jumped and bounced in his ribcage. He smiled, too. "Just wanted to show my wife how much I love her," he said, taking the few steps needed to join her. He nuzzled her neck and wrapped his arms around her waist, propping his head on her shoulder. "Wait, am I allowed to do that? Or do I have to call and set up an appointment with you for even something as basic as bringing you flowers?"

Maryssa giggled. She playfully smacked his forearm, tightening his arms around her. Andy grinned. Maryssa turned around and pecked him softly before she sauntered back towards her desk. She began to clean out the papers messily spread about, evermore radiant. Jesus, Maryssa was so fucking beautiful when she was happy.

Beautiful all the time—but especially like this. Especially when I'm the reason.

"I don't see any food with you. Did you come by just to say hello? You have to pick up Flynn from preschool, right?"

Crossing the distance between them again, Andy wound his arms around her as he had moments earlier, kissing the back of her ear. He held back his grin as she shuddered.

"Mmm. In a bit," he murmured, dragging his lips down her neck.

Maryssa giggled and tried to step out of his grasp in order to put some papers away where they belonged, but Andy instantly caged her in, forbidding her escape. Her breath hitched and Andy burned harder with desire.

He was pretty sure that he would have smiled if he hadn't gotten so worked up at the mere sound alone.

Andy mouthed the back of her neck, the crook of it where it met her shoulder, and tasted her skin with his tongue. He scraped his teeth over the wet spot, needing to make sure his intentions were clear.

Maryssa's breathing got heavier. Andy's belly churned. He'd bet anything that her cheeks were flaming red, right now.

"Not just to say hello, Maryssa," he murmured, slipping a hand under her shirt. He felt up her warm skin. "For this, too."

Maryssa hummed and arched her neck for more. She closed her eyes, breaths growing even choppier.

Andy smiled. Good. So she had been feeling the effects of their dry spell, too.

She reached back to cup his chin, the faintest moan leaving her. "Oh... Is this what the flowers were for?" she murmured.

Andy snorted—wanted to laugh, really. Only he was too full of lust. Too worked up to be able to manage. He merely continued to mouth wet kisses where he could reach. Maryssa's fingers tightened around his nape.

Only Maryssa could ask such a naive question. She was so laughably innocent in the eyes of many, strict of a boss as she could be. His wife was known to be kind and gentle, the perfect picture of a loving mother and dedicated wife... unless you screwed up when it came to her company. *Cook with Maryssa* was her long-and-hard-fought dream, one she'd had for over a decade. Maryssa would tear even Andy apart if he dared do anything to it.

God, Andy loved his wife so much. She was amazing.

"When have I ever used flowers as a way to get you to have sex with me? I just felt like getting you flowers today, babe."

He raked his teeth over her neck, pressing his fingers against her hip as he pushed his hard cock up against her ass. She moaned and blushed, but still, ground back against him.

Yeah. Definitely haven't been the only one missing this.

"Andy... I know it's been a while but... my office..."

Her mouth was saying one thing, but her body another. Something differently entirely, really. It pulled him closer, her ass rolling slowly against his cock... as though it was trying to pull any friction it could from the connection.

"Your blinds are shut. Your door is shut. I've been here enough times to know that no one ever bothers you when the door is closed," he murmured, mouthing her neck. Her breath quickened and he bit down on her skin hard enough to make her gasp. He groaned. "All we need to do is keep as quiet as we can... Come on, Maryssa. It's been seventy-one days. Don't tell me you don't feel it too..." He slipped his hand down her side, unzipped her tight-fitting pencil skirt. Andy dropped to his knees and mouthed the skin revealed to him.

Maryssa whimpered, grabbing his hair tightly. She delved both her hands through his locks, pulling at them softly. "God, Andy... I..."

The way she said his name had him rising up once more, spinning her around to capture her mouth in a hot, sensual kiss that he would bet probably made her toes curl. At least, his did. "Maryssa... Please..."

Maryssa deepened the kiss and wrapped herself around him, pushing his hardness closer between her thighs. Andy groaned, hands spanning her form and drawing little sounds from her as he squeezed this body of hers that he loved so much, *missed* so much. He loved the fact that she had actual meat on her bones—that touching her was never hard, never bony. She was all softness and curves, all velvet skin, and warmth. She had the best damn body he'd ever set his hands on.

Just kissing her already, Andy felt like he was on fire. He burned for her. Yearned for her. The fact that she was his wife never failed to amaze him every day. How was it that he was able to keep her? To make her so happy? To have her love so genuine and earnest? He was the luckiest man alive.

And the horniest, right now.

"What's it going to be, Maryssa? Are you going to allow us to take the next fifteen minutes or so to fuck like we haven't been able to in over two months? Are you going to let me bend you over that desk and make you moan so much you'll have to muffle them with your hand?" Andy asked. "Cause' I want to, Maryssa. I really want to. I want to, *so much*." He dragged in another hard kiss, his brow furrowed. His hand slipped underneath her tight bra to grab her breast. He growled. "Don't you miss my cock inside you? Rubbing parts of you that you didn't even know existed before we found each other? Don't you miss how good it felt when I came inside of you? How hot my cum was for you?"

Maryssa moaned, kissing him harder. She squeezed her thighs around him, creating friction between them that was heavenly for their pent-up lust and sexual frustration.

"I miss trying for another baby," Andy murmured, running both hands down to her ass. He squeezed firmly, groaning. "God, I miss filling you up so much. Until I knew I couldn't fill you up another inch..."

That was another thing that made it worse. Before their sexless streak, they'd recently decided to start trying for another baby now that Flynn was old enough to attend school. They felt ready to expand their family a little more, felt like they had a great handle on parenting and would be ready to face the challenge of another child— until the board of directors decided that Maryssa's company was ready for an extension, and that they wanted to do it now.

It had been cruel for the world to build up his excitement so much only to take it away.

Dipping his hands beneath her skirt, Andy felt the heaven that was the plushness of her thighs, his chest rumbling with a groan. Fuck, he wanted them wrapped around his head right now. He missed going down on Maryssa so much. But did they even have the time? Did either of them even have the patience for it?

"God, Maryssa… You have no idea how much my cock missed you. How much *I* missed you. How many times a day I think about you naked, wonder if you might be doing the same…" He licked her ear with his tongue, sucking the sensitive part of it at the back and slipping his hands underneath her panties to feel her ass directly. He let his eyes fall shut, cheeks burning. "Wonder how wet your pussy might be for me. If you were ever touching yourself. Right here, even. In that very bathroom. Fantasizing about having me between your thighs, eating you out until I left you breathless like I do every time. Every day, I think about how much I want that tight pussy wrapped around my cock, how much I want to taste it on my tongue…"

"Andy, please… *please*…"

Andy's blood soared right out of his head and towards his dick. He growled, taking one of her dainty little hands to press over his pants right where his stiff girth was. Maryssa moaned, loud enough that he clasped his hand over her mouth. Her eyes glazed over, tongue darted out to taste his hand. Andy twitched and was sure Maryssa felt it. The way such fire swept over her features guaranteed that much.

Seemingly unable to help herself, Maryssa scrambled to undo the opening of his jeans, diving her hand past the waistband of both his pants and underwear. Andy sucked in a breath, a rush of bliss flashing across his spine as her warm fingers wrapped around his rock-hard cock. He fought back against the urge to close his eyes, overcome with the sensation.

Fuck, he'd missed this. Missed those perfect fingers wrapped around him, expert in their knowledge and softer than his own could ever be. Andy couldn't wait to re-familiarize himself with her wet, perfect cunt.

"Jesus, you're so hard," Maryssa gasped, reacquainting herself with the feel of him in her small hands. Her lips twitched as she ran her thumb over the head of him and felt his precum leak out, but Andy suspected she was the same as him—unable to truly muster up a smile because of all her yearning and desire.

His eyes slipped shut, hips bucking against her hand. "Of course I'm hard. I've been hard for weeks," he groaned. "Waiting for us to make time again..."

"God, Andy... I'm sorry. I'm sorry I've been making you wait so much," she said, moving her hand on him with just the pressure he liked best. Jesus, God fucking bless his wife for having never forgotten his preferences.

Andy kissed her hard. He tangled his fingers in her hair, tugging possessively. "Don't be sorry," he rasped, biting her lip. "Never be sorry for taking care of your dream. I want you to be happy. Always." He let out a brief, strangled laugh. "Even if my dick hates me for it sometimes."

"Not right now it doesn't," she retorted back breathlessly, and they both laughed.

He pushed her down so her back was on the desk and began unbuttoning her blouse. At every inch of skin revealed, Andy hungrily tasted it, his chest rumbling as Maryssa moaned and wrapped her legs around him. Andy barely had the sense to understand the encouraging things she murmured, too worked up, simply knowing this was happening at last.

He was going to fuck his wife. In her office. After seventy-one days without sex. He was finally going to see her cum again.

The thought had him groaning, teeth raking against her nipple over her pretty bra. He cupped both swells of her wonderful breasts. That was another thing with her. She had the most wonderful fucking tits he'd ever seen and touched in this world. The tits of his dreams. Her whole fucking body was a godsend.

They were both startled when her office phone rang, one of them moaning a complaint. Andy wasn't sure who. Maybe they both had.

Ever so dutiful in her role, though, Maryssa shifted and rolled on her desk so she could answer, giving Andy a torturous view of her ass in her pretty panties. Her skirt was still all bunched up high over her tummy, so tight that Andy was sure it had to be uncomfortable.

"Maryssa Lafont speaking."

Professional. Incredibly. Andy was honestly impressed. He was sure if he tried speaking right now, he'd sound like a wolven beast or something. That's how full of desire he felt.

As if to prove that point, Andy reached out instinctively and grabbed the hem of her unzipped, bunched-up skirt. He started pulling it down, hungry to see her out of it.

Maryssa smacked away one of his hands, briefly throwing him a glare as she gestured to give her one minute. Andy bit back a lecherous grin.

He didn't listen.

"Oh. Yes, two o'clock. That's right. I have it marked down," Maryssa went on, eyes falling shut. She bit her own lip as he dragged down her skirt over her hips and down her legs, briefly clasping a hand over her mouth. "And one at three-thirty as well. Yes. Thank you, Azah. Enjoy your lunch now, okay?"

The second she hung up, Andy's mouth was on her ass, biting it. Maryssa cried out, head falling against her arms. Andy palmed the span of her thick, perfect thighs, hungrily taking in the bare skin. He didn't waste another moment before sliding off her panties, too, groaning at her sweet, musky scent.

Christ, he needed to taste her so bad.

Maryssa seemed to think so as well; she ever so shyly parted her legs and whimpered, face still hidden in the crook of her arms.

"Andy… Andy, please."

Andy snapped. Snarling a string of incoherent words, he flipped her around and drew her legs over his shoulders, burying his face into her sweet, wet cunt. Maryssa gasped, throwing a hand over her mouth to bite back a cry. She snatched her hand in his hair with the other, moaning his name and pleas to keep going. Andy groaned in return, hungrily working his mouth on her clit in the way he knew she loved. He sank two fingers into her depths, his dick so painful in the restraints of his pants he wanted nothing but to reach down and relieve some delicious tension.

Still, Andy ignored it.

Not long later when Maryssa was close—or so he suspected as she started quivering and thrashing the way she always did when she was on the brink—she pulled on his hair and panted, urging him back up. Andy obliged. And though he wanted to finish her off, have her cum on his tongue and break apart right on that desk, as soon as she looked at him with her misty eyes thick with love and bliss, Andy was a goner.

He knew he'd give her anything she wanted. Anything she asked. So there was no way in hell he'd have been able to deny her what she wanted when she whimpered her next words.

"Andy, not like this… *Please*. Please, I need you. Inside me. I need you now, Andy," she said, tugging ever more insistently on his hair.

Andy was up to his feet in seconds, yanking down his pants as quickly as he could manage. When they were out of the way, he pulled his lovely wife by her hips until she was hanging off the edge of her desk. He licked his lips, the blood roaring in his ears growing even louder as she wrapped her legs around him tightly, dragging their lower halves as close as she could get them.

Somehow, it tore a smile out of him. She wanted him to be inside her just as bad as he wanted to. She was just as desperate to be close to him as he was to her. She'd been just as affected by their dry spell, emotionally and physically.

Andy wasn't going to let it go on for a single moment longer.

Taking his cock in hand, Andy guided himself to her warm, wet opening, heart pounding away like drums. They both held their breath when he started pushing in, Maryssa even arching her back and jerking him closer with her legs in an attempt to push more of his girth inside. It worked a little.

Andy groaned, thrusting shallowly until he was deeply seated within her perfect pussy. His eyes swept shut briefly, waves of bliss rolling over him. He let out a string of curses once he opened them again and met his wife's gaze. She hadn't looked this turned on in ages—perhaps in forever. Her eyes blazed like a wildfire, pooling lust so hot in his stomach that it felt like lava.

The sight alone had him picking up his pace. Andy pulled her up to meld their mouths together, threading a hand into her beautiful hair. Maryssa grabbed his hips, silently begging for more as she kissed him back harder and dug her nails into his skin. Andy obliged, moving his hips in quick little pounds that had her moaning, panting, moving desperately to try and meet his thrusts.

"Andy... *Andy*, I missed you so much," she gasped between hot, fevered kisses, dropping both hands down to his ass. "God, I missed you. Oh *God*, I really missed you."

Andy groaned. He broke from her and bit down on her neck, fucking her harder.

"Yeah?" he rasped, sliding his palm over her breast. He squeezed it aggressively. Hungrily. "D'you miss me—or the way my cock feels inside you? I bet you just missed the way it makes you moan. How good it fucks your wet little cunt. Look at how much it's dripping for me. I can feel how slick you are. You're probably dripping on your office floor." Keeping her close with his other hand, he leveraged himself with her weight to maintain the pace and strength of his thrusts. He licked his lips. "Is that what you want, Maryssa? For me to fuck you so good that you drip all over your pretty little office floors, so your cleaning crew finds out their boss came all over her desk? You dirty minx. I bet that's what you want. I bet you want to squeeze all the cum from my cock and have it drip all over the floor so everyone can know how filthy you can be. So they stop seeing you as the sweet, innocent CEO. So they can take you seriously like you wish they would…"

"No," Maryssa whined, burying her face in his neck. She quivered around him and jerked towards him to meet his thrusts, though, and Andy knew that meant the idea seriously turned her on.

"I'd never—That's so—"

She cut herself off and buried herself closer, so much he would bet anything that she was flushed from ear to ear. Still, she kept moaning, meeting his thrusts eagerly, too needy to let her embarrassment stop her.

Before long, Maryssa began nipping his ear, panting. She whimpered, biting him hard enough to make him hiss. "I swear, you have such—Such a dirty mouth," she gasped, tongue coming out to taste his lobe.

Andy ground against her roughly, tearing a cry from her mouth. Maryssa yanked him closer by his ass, one hand flying out to the edge of the desk to brace herself against it. Andy grinned devilishly, pride swelling within him. Drawing back to catch the look on her face, he captured her lips with his in a feverish kiss, dizzy. He groaned as her walls pulsed and closed in on him—a tale-tell sign that she was close.

"You love this dirty mouth," he whispered, tugging her lip with his teeth. "You love it so much you're about to cum right now. Like you always do. I can feel how much you love it when I talk dirty to you, honey."

Maryssa's breath caught, the red on her cheeks darkening to an even more gorgeous shade. Andy's mouth curled into a grin. He kissed her once more, tugging her body even further off the desk until she was practically hanging off. He grabbed both of her warm, soft thighs, thrusting with even more fervor.

The cry Maryssa let out right then was so sharp even into their kiss that Andy could only be thankful that his mouth had muffled most of the sound. Someone would have surely heard her if it hadn't—and Andy couldn't even fathom the idea of being interrupted while he was about to make his wife cum for the first time in much too long.

Troubled by the thought, Andy braced one hand against her desk, too, and moved faster, harder. The sturdy piece of furniture began to rattle with violent force, so much that some stacks of paper and a plastic cup of pens fell off. Andy didn't allow himself to care, though. He panted and groaned, losing himself to his pleasure. Mind clouding up with bliss, he focused on nothing but holding out for Maryssa—needing her to cum more than anything else. More than himself.

It didn't take long. Maryssa dipped her hips and curved her back to get an angle she wanted, and that was it. Half a dozen thrusts and she crumbled into a mess of muffled cries, trembling. She came apart so beautifully that Andy quickly found himself wishing he could have seen the look on her face. With a hard bite to his shoulder—hard enough she might have drawn blood—she muffled a series of high, carnal sounds that went right to his cock.

They sent him tumbling over the edge with her, blinding his vision white.

Together they ground out their blissful releases and held each other close. Wanting to prolong the intimacy of the moment and ensure every drop of his cum filled her as deeply as possible. Or so Andy believed.

His heart melted with the weight of all his love. "Fuck, Maryssa… I missed you so much. Missed being close to you like this," he murmured, drawing back to lock gazes with her. He thumbed her cheek, such softness and warmth filling his heart, and smiled, capturing her lips the most sentimental kiss. "Missed filling you with my cum. Did you feel how much I gave you? That's only for you, honey. No one's ever made me cum like that before. Best pussy I ever had."

Maryssa seemed to shudder, but still she pouted against his mouth. She broke away and buried her face in his neck, holding him tight. "Okay, enough with the dirty talk," she mumbled. "I already came. No need to work me up again."

Andy chuckled, kissing her collarbone and sighing blissfully. He propped her back more comfortably against the desk, figuring the edge digging into her so much probably wasn't very comfortable, and smiled. Maryssa seemed to appreciate it—even though the movement had him slipping out. She sighed and kissed him slowly.

"You love it," Andy murmured between a kiss. "But fair enough. Sorry, I'll stop now." With one last kiss, he swept her beautiful hair over her shoulder. His heart was so full as he stared at her. He pressed his forehead against hers, keeping their gazes locked. "I love you. And I really did miss you. Not just the sex. You've been so busy lately…" He trailed out, and shook his head against hers. "No, *we've* been so busy. I'm proud of you. I never want you to feel bad about putting your career before our sex life."

Her lips curved, at first just a little. But then suddenly, with such tenderness and love that it was breathtaking to watch, they quirked further up into a full, utterly exquisite smile. Andy's heart skipped a beat. His mouth parted.

Christ, his wife was so beautiful. Time and time again, it never failed to escape Andy how lucky he was to have Maryssa at his side. Amazing inside and out. She was ten times the person he could ever hope to be.

Maryssa cupped his jaw with her slim fingers, pulling him in for a sweet kiss. Andy's heart thundered, a blush spreading to his cheeks the moment she lowered her hand on his chest, to the space over his heart. She smiled even wider, pressing their heads together again. She was so damn lovely.

"I love you, too, Andy. So much." She paused. She tucked a lock of hair behind her ear, her flushed cheeks turning a shade redder. "But um… Do you think you could maybe help me make all this look presentable again? It's… well, kind of cluttered. And my legs are shaky."

Because you've been well-fucked, Andy thought, and didn't realize he was grinning until Maryssa shot him a dangerous—if still somehow amused—look. Andy laughed, too pleased with himself. Maryssa shook her head and smiled, muttering something under her breath he didn't hear. Still snickering, Andy kissed the top of her head before bending down and picking up her skirt and panties for her. He handed them back out.

"Course'. Anything for my wife." Crouching back down for his pants, he pulled them on, too. "Just need to clean up first. Do you want me to get you some tissues or toilet paper from the bathroom while I'm at it?"

Smiling brighter, Maryssa nodded. She pecked him and hopped off the desk to begin re-dressing, legs indeed a little wobbly. The sight swelled the silliest but most incredible pride inside his chest. He hurried off towards the bathroom, shoulders high and straightened.

When Andy came back, Maryssa was buttoning up her blouse and still skirt-less, presumably so he could help clean up the mess between her legs. She looked back when she heard the bathroom door and smiled. Tucking her hair behind her ear, she finished buttoning up her blouse.

"Thank you, sweetie," she said when he made his way to her, stretching out a hand to accept the items.

Andy didn't hand them over, though. He simply dropped down to his knees and carefully started wiping her down with the toilet paper he'd run through water, cleaning up any evidence of their encounter. The appreciative hand Maryssa put on his head swelled tenderness inside him, enough that he couldn't resist wrapping his arms around her and burying his face in her belly.

"Think we did it this time?" he murmured, closing his eyes.

Maryssa threaded her hand in his hair. Her other cupped the back of his neck, lovingly. She sighed, contently. "I hope so, Andy. I really hope so."

Andy heaved a long breath, pressing his lips over her stomach where their child might be. He smiled and looked up at his amazing wife. "Man, I really hope we have a girl this time. Don't you?"

Maryssa blinked quickly, and then she laughed. "What, you want to play teatime with a bunch of stuffed animals?"

Andy grinned. "Sounds amazing. Will you bake us cookies?"

Maryssa's laughter quickly died, stunned silence replacing it. Then, she smiled, so damn beautifully his heart actually hurt seeing it. She urged him up wordlessly; Andy obeyed. Maryssa wrapped her arms around him, kissing him slow and sweetly.

"For teatime with our little girl? Always."

Andy's heart had never felt so full.

Story 5 - Cherry Chapstick Lips (First time lesbian)

Sophie stirred awake to her head pounding, beating against her temples like a tribal drum in the midst of a ceremonial dance, powerful like no other instrument could be. But her hangover was far from anything to be celebrated or admired, however—especially with how nauseous it was making her.

What was cause for celebration, though, were the arms wrapped around her right now: dark brown, slim, and unbearably familiar. So beautiful in contrast to Sophie's pale, creamy skin. Undoubtedly, Sophie knew who these arms belonged to. They were Hazel's, her roommate.

Sophie wanted to groan. She should have realized that getting trashed with Hazel when she had the biggest lady-boner for her would end up with the two of them passed out in bed. Cuddling. Especially since she and Hazel had been flirting since the first day they met. (It felt like flirting to her, anyway. With girls, it could be so difficult to tell when teasing banter carried more weight.)

It didn't help that the two of them had even made out on a few occasions—mostly when they were tipsy on Natty Light and screwdrivers, surrounded by equally tipsy college students. The two of them had always brushed it off, though. Or, well, Sophie did to be sure. She'd never known how Hazel felt about it all. Sophie always blamed it on the alcohol and Hazel never seemed to disagree, so if neither of them attempted to bring it up even now, then surely it meant that Hazel was cool with it, too, right?

Yet, Sophie's stomach still twisted uncomfortably at the thought. Whether with doubt or worry—or something else. Something like longing. It wasn't quite that she wanted to *be* with Hazel, but Sophie still wanted it to mean more, be more, than drunken fumbling. She didn't want for either of them to have to take vodka doubling as a cleaning agent to tempt them to kiss the other. Sophie certainly didn't need it, anyway. She never wanted to go back to pretending her attraction to girls wasn't real.

"I told you to buy blackout curtains and better blinds," Hazel mumbled behind her, eliciting a flinch from Sophie. "These are so shitty they barely keep any light out."

Sophie swallowed the lump in her throat. "You're just a vampire," she replied.

Hazel laughed, the sound rough with sleep. "No, you simply can't manage to pick out any quality products—like, ever."

Sophie's lips twitched but she feigned a gasp. She poked Hazel's arm too gently to be anything but playful. "Hey! Do not."

"Do too."

Hazel poked her back—a bit less gently—and Sophie yelped. But when Hazel's lips curved into a smile, her brown eyes softening, she couldn't help smiling, too.

"Remind me... who was it that complimented the dining table that I picked out yesterday?" Sophie asked, wiggling in Hazel's hold until she was facing her. She tapped a finger to her lips. "Oh, right. You."

Hazel snorted. "You did *not* pick that out. Your mom did." She rolled her eyes.

"So I did. By proxy. *Burn.*"

Hazel stared at her, deeply unimpressed. "What year is it, 2010? Who even says 'burn' anymore?"

"Only cool people," Sophie quipped. She started to grin but winced as her head started throbbing harder, fingers coming to rub at her temples. "Ugh. Please tell me you have a hangover this time."

Hazel's mouth lifted at the corners. "You want me to lie to you?"

Sophie groaned, moving her hand across her eyes. It didn't actually help to lessen her headache, but at least it blocked out the sunlight. Maybe Hazel had a point about the blinds.

"Seriously? What the fuck. That is so unfair. Why do you never get them? You're not human."

"Great genes, baby."

Sophie erupted into giggles, her cheeks reddening. Her amusement faded quickly when her temples pulsed more violently, protesting the laugh. It was still worth the pain, though. Kidding around with Hazel trumped any hangover, no matter how awful. "Right. Screw you. Shut up now or you'll make my head explode."

"I'm not the one who refused water when the bartender offered it to you, and I didn't make you drink all those tequila shots," Hazel reminded her.

"You didn't stop me either," Sophie muttered.

Hazel huffed. "Honey, I'm not your mom. I didn't pick out that dining table. Don't go blaming me. Take responsibility for your own choices."

Sophie's lips quirked up again, fondness rushing through her heart. God, that cheeky, no-nonsense demeanor. Sophie loved it. It could make Hazel so unbelievably attractive, sometimes. But then, she always was.

Sophie peered down at Hazel's shirt, drawn in by the cartoon print of Tweety Bird. They were both in pajamas, but as far as Sophie could recall, they had gone to bed dressed in their club clothes. It was hard to forget falling asleep in a skintight bodycon dress that cut off her circulation, and Sophie couldn't remember waking up and changing into her pajamas. Only that they'd watched *Dirty Grandpa* and eaten leftover Chinese food. Had she and Hazel made out before they crashed? Had they undressed each other? Had they had *sex*?

Oh, God. I hope we didn't have sex, Sophie thought. Her first time with a woman and she'd have no memory of it? That was a mortifying concept—and concerning. If she'd been wasted enough to blackout then she was way too drunk to be having sex and that applied to Hazel, too.

"I swear I can see the wheels spinning in your head. What are you overthinking this time?" Hazel asked.

Sophie could feel her cheeks burning hotter. "Um. Nothing."

"Liar."

"Am not!"

"Then why are you staring at Tweety bird like your brain is about to fry a circuit?"

"I wasn't—" Sophie kept her mouth shut. Okay, she was. Hazel wasn't blind *or* crazy, and as a Black woman, she particularly hated when people tried to make her believe otherwise.

Sophie relented with a sigh. "I'm just... trying to puzzle something out."

"Uh-huh." Hazel stared at her. That was Sophie's cue to go on.

She ran a hand over her face. "We slept in the same bed."

"Yep."

"In our pajamas."

"Mhm." None of this seemed to bother Hazel, as though this was an everyday thing with them—and it very well wasn't.

Sophie bit her tongue. "But last I can remember, we weren't *in* our pajamas when we went to bed, Hazel."

"The first time, yeah," Hazel replied, nonchalantly stretching out her arms over her head.

"The firs—" Sophie sucked in a breath. She rubbed her forehead and rolled on her back. "Did we sleep together? Like…" Sophie gestured vaguely with her hands, like she was playing the world's most awkward game of charades.

Apparently, she wasn't very good at it because Hazel tilted her head and asked, brow raised, "What is that supposed to be?"

"Oh, God. You know what—Never mind!"

"Was that supposed to mean *sex*?"

"Jesus Christ. Just—Just forget about i—" Sophie clammed up, nausea returning and gripping her violently. Oh, *shit*. "I'm gonna throw up," she warned with a near-whimper, scrambling out of bed and towards their shared bathroom.

She barely made it to the toilet before dropping to her knees and heaving all of last night's Chinese food. Sophie's world blurred over, a mess of stinky vomit that still smelled a bit like tequila, tears blurring her vision, and thoughts of regret running rampant across her mind.

She thought she heard someone saying something too, but she wasn't sure, too focused on throwing her whole life up.

When it was over, she realized someone was holding her hair. Hazel, definitely—because who else could it be?

This had to be the unsexiest thing ever. "Why do you have to keep seeing me at my worst?" Sophie asked, bemoaning her luck. Figures that the first night she slept in the same bed as her crush, a hangover would ruin everything. Oh well. At least she felt better already. Despite the still-lingering headache, spilling her guts out seemed to have helped her overall state.

Hazel snorted. "Hello? We live together."

"Remind me why again?"

"You do my laundry."

The words left her mouth so naturally that Sophie's head snapped up to throw her roommate a dirty look. Her cheeks warmed as Hazel smirked back. "Har har. Very funny," Sophie said, rolling her eyes.

Hazel puffed out a *psh* noise and replied, "So are you. You know why we moved in together after leaving our dorm. We're attached at the hip."

Sophie grumbled. "Yeah, I know. Sorry. Can you get me a glass of water?"

Hazel made it to the kitchen and back, bearing the promised water, in less than a minute. She handed Sophie the cup, but Sophie was so dizzy that when she accepted it, her fingers shook so badly that half the contents spilled on her shirt.

"Did you forget how to drink, too?" Hazel asked, sniggering.

"Hazel," Sophie whined. "Shut up."

"Here, let me help you get that off."

Sophie nodded, blushing, and let Hazel help her out. Part of her was a little panicked; though Hazel had to know that Sophie wasn't wearing a bra, and Sophie was sure she had seen many breasts in her life and never blinked an eye, something about right now still felt so different. They weren't just two women changing in the locker room or walking in on the other naked in the public dorm showers. They were Sophie and Hazel, two openly bisexual girls who had made out on multiple occasions and were clearly attracted to each other—and they had just slept in the same bed, cuddling all night.

Once the shirt was off, Sophie's nipples stiffened instantly from the chilliness of the room. She held her breath, watching Hazel's gaze dip to her chest. Sophie was sure she wasn't imagining things as Hazel's pale, almost golden eyes ignited with desire. Her insides practically melted. She swore she even saw Hazel's tongue peek out and run subtly over her lips.

She wanted to tease Hazel. Wanted to snap her out of her reverie and ask her if she liked what she was seeing. But Hazel was staring at her with such heat that she was finding it hard to breathe. How cliche was that?

"You know you have an amazing rack, right?" Hazel said.

Sophie's mouth dried. Her cheeks turned redder. Still, she lifted her chin with feigned confidence and put a hand on her hip. "They're pretty good, yeah. Nothing compared to yours, though."

Hazel's lips twitched higher. Her brow rose as if she was challenged. And maybe she was, Sophie admitted.

And so she nodded, as though it was her whole point. "Maybe you should take off your shirt too and we could have a more direct comparison."

Hazel's not-quite-golden eyes gleamed brighter. They bore into her own, burning as though they could set fire to anything they touched, should they want to. They fell down and carefully mapped out her breasts again, their hunger growing. Like she wanted to put her mouth on Sophie's nipples and memorize their shape with her tongue, over and over again.

Sophie nearly shivered at the thought alone. *Do it. I dare you. Please.*

"Maybe," Hazel said, eyes flickering up to hers again. "That's not a bad idea at all."

Sophie's brain barely had the time to process the words before Hazel asked, "You know what? Why don't you take it off for me?"

Through all their years knowing each other, Sophie had always thought Hazel's smirks were sexy. But the one that formed on her lips right now? The one so cocky and full of silent, repressed desire—all of which at this very moment was solely meant for her? It had her stomach flipping, the warm space between her legs dampening instantly.

She gawked and stood so very still as Hazel stepped closer, guiding Sophie's hands to the hem of her pajama shirt. She lifted it up some, bunching it all up around her hips. She stared expectantly at Sophie with an air of confidence Sophie knew she could never have. Not like her.

"Well?" Hazel urged, quirking her brow.

A fire rose in Sophie's chest, her competitive side. She grasped Hazel's hips briefly, eyes narrowing. She quickly yanked Hazel's shirt off, her hands instinctively settling on her newly bared breasts.

This is it, isn't it? This is finally happening, Sophie thought, amazed. *Two years of yearning for her and not wanting to ruin the close friendship we have, and we're actually facing all this sexual tension between us.*

Sophie wasn't sure whether or not this was a good idea. She loved Hazel but she wasn't *in love* with her. She didn't know if Hazel felt the same, too, but it was likely that she wasn't in love with Sophie either. She had seen Hazel in love. It was nothing like this. But was it really such a smart thing for two close friends to sleep together when they lived together?

I'm sleeping with Zeke all the time and he's my best friend. Neither of us have any feelings for each other. So why should this be any different? Because she's a girl?

Sophie shook her head, earning herself an amused look from Hazel. She smiled cheekily, uttering a quick, "Sorry—overthinking brain again."

Hazel huffed, her eyes crinkling at the corners. She pushed Sophie's hands closer, squeezing them around her fantastic breasts. "Stop thinking so much and touch me already."

Sophie struggled not to grin, circling both of her dark nipples before stepping away. She put a finger up before Hazel could protest. "Give me a minute to brush my teeth and use some mouthwash? I don't think anyone wants to kiss someone with hangover breath."

Hazel laughed, moving aside to allow her to get to the sink. "Okay, yeah."

Beaming, Sophie proceeded to the tiny washbasin, gathering her things. She couldn't believe she was about to do this. Not ten minutes ago, she was hurling over the toilet with a hangover so strong she could barely think. But now? Now her whole body felt utterly consumed and overtaken by lust, only a faint headache lingering in the background—easily ignored. On any other day, Sophie might have spent a good few hours in bed, vowing never to drink again. But not today.

Not today.

Expecting Hazel to get out and maybe fetch them some coffee or possibly even surprise her naked in bed, Sophie was startled to find her instead wrapping her arms around her waist, lips smoothing over her skin to plant slow, delightful kisses on her shoulder. Those lips made a path to her neck, hands cupping the weight of her breasts, getting to know their curves before they started playing with her hard peaks.

Sophie let out a shuddering breath and strangled hum, sagging back into Hazel and nearly choking on her toothbrush.

Hazel cracked up, exclaiming something like, "Come on, girl, don't die on me now. We're just getting to the good stuff."

Sophie had never been motivated to brush her teeth so fast in her life.

By the time she was finished barely half a minute later, she was in all but her underwear all thanks to Hazel and her wonderful hands. Hazel was still kissing her neck, holding one of Sophie's breasts in her hand while the other hand busied itself between her thighs. It had been doing wondrous work rubbing Sophie's cunt over last night's sexy, barely-there thong—which was considerably damp at this point.

It was driving Sophie insane. But something about all this was making her nervous—no, no... more like *clueless*. She'd done all this so many times with a man before today, but right now, with Hazel? Everything felt so different. New—but all in familiar ways, as odd as that sounded. Did all women like to be kissed behind the ear as she did? Did Hazel? Did they all like their clit rubbed in circles?

Probably not, right?

"Earth to Hazel. There are those gears again," Hazel hummed, nipping her earlobe. "What are you overthinking now, babe?"

Turning around in her arms, Sophie wrapped her arms around Hazel's neck and drew her into a long kiss. Her lips always tasted so good. Soft and never dry, the faint flavor of honey-melon always clinging to them. Was it Hazel's body wash? Her shampoo? Sophie would have to check what kind she used the next time she took a shower. Hazel always carried such an amazing smell, amazing everything—which was better than all these college men who consistently sprayed themselves with Axe rather than bathed.

"Honey, what's wrong?" Hazel said, gently breaking away from her. "You are so in your head. What's going on? Are you a virgin?"

Sophie gaped. "What? Are you kidding me? You heard me have sex like three days ago when Zeke was here!" she exclaimed, flustered. Like, seriously! How could she even say that? Sophie ran a hand through her hair, slowly becoming more red-faced. "That is legitimately the stupidest question I think you've ever asked me."

Hazel's brow lifted, and she tugged her closer by her hips. "Okay, let me rephrase that. Are you a virgin *when it comes to lesbian sex?*"

Sophie's mind went blank, if only for a few seconds. Her mouth dropped open wider—which she didn't even know was possible. She couldn't even find her voice; a good thing, as Sophie found there was nothing more that she wanted than to vehemently deny Hazel's assumption. Even if it was true.

She didn't really understand why.

Hazel's face softened with sympathy and Sophie winced. Letting out a heavy sigh, her shoulders slumped, and she ran her hands over her furiously blushing face, recognizing when she was defeated. "...Yes. Okay? I've made out with tons of girls before—and you know this, you've been one of them! —but I've never... well, never slept with one. Or gone further than making out. So..."

Sophie tried to cross her arms and avoid Hazel's gaze, but Hazel wouldn't let her. She stopped Sophie in her tracks and trapped her back against the counter, her eyes gleaming. God, she was close. So close that Sophie could feel her breath, could easily just lean forward and take Hazel's lips with her own.

"Cute," Hazel murmured. "Sophie, it's not a big deal that you are. I'm not a guy. As far as I know, most women don't cower away from other women who have only slept with the opposite sex. I certainly don't. If anything, I'm excited to show you how great lesbian sex is."

Lesbian sex. There it was again. Sophie was nervous but it seemed like every time she heard the word *sex* and *lesbian* coming from Hazel's mouth, she grew ever more excited. Sex. Lesbian sex. With Hazel. Her longtime crush—if only for fantasies.

She was getting wetter and wetter simply thinking about it.

Getting ever more riled up, Sophie surged forward, kissing Hazel with all of the dizzying lust within her. Hazel made a sound of surprise but kissed her back, never wasting another moment to run her hands all over Sophie's body. Sophie was of a similar mind, hungrily exploring Hazel's body as though she never had before, paying particular attention to her ass and amazing breasts.

Never breaking away, Hazel started guiding her out of her bathroom and towards their living room, where they collapsed on the couch together. Hazel settled on top of her, caressing her thighs and the edges of Sophie's racy thong. Sophie could only be glad she'd decided to wear sexy underwear when going out clubbing last night. And even though she always knew Hazel would be more of a top, she still found herself surprised by the amount of initiative Hazel took.

There was no hesitation on her part. Hazel knew what she was doing and what she was going to do next. There was no uncertainty, no cluelessness. She was clearly experienced—well-versed in the knowledge of handling a woman.

That, in particular, became very clear when Hazel's hand slipped down her panties and started touching the most sensitive part of her. Sophie gasped into their kiss, deepening it and raking her fingers through Hazel's frizzy hair. Hazel murmured something Sophie didn't have the brains to process, possibly dirty words or perhaps a question about what she liked.

All that Sophie had the brains to process was the pleasure—brought to her by Hazel's wonderful fingers. She couldn't believe how different it felt to be touched by another woman. Her touch was so good—so damn *fucking fantastic*. Men's fingers were nearly always more reckless, unless they already knew what their partners liked, and they touched with a sort of urgency, like speed was the only technique to her pleasure.

It wasn't. And Hazel knew that. Hazel was the complete opposite, even, touching her exquisitely slowly but with unhurried, hard rubs that had Sophie shuddering again and again. All she could do was kiss Hazel, and kiss her some more. She opened her thighs wider to give Hazel more access— embarrassingly often. So much that it was obscene and, worse, desperate. But somehow, that only made it better.

Until one abrupt moment, Hazel's fingers stopped moving. Sophie's mind kept spinning—unpleasantly, now.

"Do you like fingering?" she asked as she pulled away from their kiss. She radiated such smugness that Sophie figured she must have mourned the loss of friction with a needy noise or something.

God, she could barely think because of how badly her head was spinning right now. "Um—Yeah. I mean—when done right, that is. I mean—" Sophie reddened, turning crimson all the way up to her roots and snapping her mouth shut. *Fuck. I can't believe I—When done right? Did I really have to add that?*

She could have instead clarified that she preferred it a certain way—saying it like *that* was a one-way ticket to offending someone.

If Hazel was annoyed, she didn't show it. Her eyes merely glinted. "Don't worry about that, honey. When you've been with as many women as I have, you *know* how to use your fingers."

"How many women have you been with?" Sophie asked, curious.

Hazel tilted her head, frowning. "Is that really important right now?"

"I guess not..." Sophie mumbled. She gasped and arched her back when Hazel started stroking her once more, her hands taking a mind of their own and caressing Hazel's back, her shoulders... all the way down to her breasts. She dug her teeth down into her lip, winding both arms soundly around Hazel's neck and pushing up to kiss her. "You can—Yeah. Whenever."

Hazel snickered against her mouth. "Eager now, are we?"

Sophie gaped. "You're the one who asked!" she protested.

"I'm not in any hurry," Hazel said, her eyes gleaming. "Seems like you are, though."

"I—Your hand is in my underwear. *On my clit*. Of course I'm a little worked up and eager!" Puffing her cheeks, Sophie buried her face in Hazel's neck to kiss and bite where she could. She threaded her fingers through Hazel's gorgeous hair again, scratching her nails against her scalp punishingly.

A smile lifted her lips when Hazel shuddered, clearly not as composed as she liked to pretend. That made Sophie feel much better for some reason.

"Okay, yeah. Maybe we've been waiting long enough to sleep together," Hazel gibed, letting out a breathless laugh. Somehow, it only served to work up Sophie even further.

Sophie locked one ankle behind Hazel's back and dragged her in for a deep kiss. "Glad I wasn't crazy and that there really was all this sexual tension between us these past two years," she panted out between two very involved kisses, goosebumps prickling her skin as Hazel's fingers inched further down, circling her entrance.

Slowly, they pushed inside and started setting up a nice, steady beat, wrenching a sweet moan out of her.

Sophie moaned when Hazel pushed her fingers in, setting up a slow, steady beat.

"What could you possibly mean?" Hazel asked, her voice wry. "We're just *friends*. Friends finger each other. That's what gal pals do."

Sophie laughed, the sound broken by gasps and little blissful noises. Hazel kissed her for it, bracing herself against her free hand and picking up the pace with the other. Sophie whimpered and tried to drag Hazel closer with the ankle around her back, only to end up throwing Hazel off her balance. Hazel crumbled flat on Sophie's body, knocking her chin against her collarbone and sending the pair of them groaning.

Apparently, Hazel was completely justified in calling her a virgin, because she hadn't been this clumsy with sex since her first time.

"Sorry..."

"You know what? Maybe we should move to the bedroom before we get too far," Hazel said, stroking her jaw and wincing. "That way if anything like this happens again, neither of us has the chance to tumble to the floor and get hurt."

"Agreed," Sophie said, grimacing as she rubbed her own injury, too.

Hazel got up first, naturally, then held out her hand. When Sophie took it, she felt how wet Hazel's fingers were—wet from her cunt. As if she needed anything to turn her on more. Hazel led her down the hall to Sophie's room, guiding without forcing. The moment they stepped inside, Hazel maneuvered her to the edge of the bed and lightly pushed her onto it. Softness settled around her, the mattress plush beneath her weight, a luxurious warmth spreading over her from head to toe.

Sophie scrambled back on the bed. She chucked off her panties while Hazel shimmied out of her pajama shorts and blue undies, briefly mourning the fact she never got to take them off Hazel. Sophie would have liked to have bitten that ass, so much fuller than hers could ever be. Her breasts were modest, but her ass lacked some serious juice. At least it didn't stop her from getting laid, though.

Hazel was over to her in seconds, hand reaching between Sophie's legs once more. Sophie propped them up on the bed and opened wide, yanking Hazel to her level for a hot kiss, full of teeth and tongue. She kept kissing Hazel with all the frenzied passion within her as Hazel slipped her fingers back inside her pussy and gradually set up a relentless pace. It tore raw sounds from Sophie's lips, most of them muffled against Hazel's mouth.

It was clear that Hazel knew what she was doing. With her fingers curved *just* to reach that spot within her that most men never found, the buildup to her orgasm was quicker. Stronger. Even compared to when she was by herself. She'd spent so many nights craving this, Hazel playing her body like a violin, and tried in vain to ease that ache on her own. Now she knew exactly how far short her fantasies fell from the real thing.

"Keep going. Just like that. Gonna cum," she puffed between a kiss, panting in staccato beats. She nipped Hazel's lush bottom lip roughly, keening a delighted cry.

Hazel didn't say anything, maintaining that punishing rhythm with expert fingers. She clearly had no plans for a magical finishing move, because she knew it wasn't necessary. A woman who could work a cunt like that could skip the bells and whistles, and besides, Sophie had told her exactly what she had to do. What she had to keep doing in order to make her come.

It didn't take her long to get there.

Crying out sharply, Sophie dropped one hand against the sheets and tightly gripped onto them, blinding white wiping her mind. She snatched Hazel by the back of her head so she could kiss her with all the ferocity her tiny body could ever contain. Whines broke through their messy, fiery exchange, but Hazel didn't seem to mind at all. In fact, judging by the smirk that Sophie felt curling Hazel's lips, she enjoyed every bit of it.

"Cum good, honey?" she asked, a little arrogantly.

It made Sophie smile—if however lopsidedly. Her smile was one that conveyed how very blissed-out and dazed she was, but it was genuine, nonetheless.

Cupping both sides of Hazel's neck, Sophie kissed her sweetly, prolonging it for as much as she could in order to silently show her appreciation. Hazel chuckled, her fingers leaving her wet cunt to travel up her thigh, side, and over one breast. She flicked Sophie's nipple, tongue meeting Sophie's own with enough heat that Sophie couldn't help whining again. She reached out to grab Hazel's ass, loving the delicious curve of it. God, she wished she had an ass like that. But Hazel probably wore it better than Sophie ever could.

She smacked one ass cheek at the thought, loving the way Hazel's breath hitched.

Sophie grinned. "Definitely not surprised that you like being spanked," she said smugly.

Hazel guffawed and bestowed her a challenging stare. "Yeah? What other kinks did you suspect that I have?"

"Is that really important right now?" Sophie teased, recalling Hazel's earlier words.

It was Hazel's turn to grin. "I guess not," she returned, just as teasingly.

Sophie rolled them over so she was on top, slanting her mouth on Hazel's for a long, all-consuming kiss. She trailed her fingers down to Hazel's neck, over her shoulders, and across her collarbone in a path towards her breasts. She broke away and left a trail of hot kisses along the same path, enveloping a hard, peaked nipple when she reached the same destination. Hoping Hazel's preferences were similar, she sucked and nipped at the tender bud much how she liked it done on hers. Briefly, she recalled Hazel sharing when she was drunk how much she loved having her nipples pinched, so Sophie did that, too.

"Not bad for a newbie," Hazel commented, breathless. Sophie glanced up to find her biting her lip, her not-quite-golden eyes so pleasure-hazed that Sophie was sure she would be blushing if it were possible. God, Hazel was always so stunning. But like this? She was even more so. "Listening to your instincts?"

"Trying out tricks that work on me… and remembering things you said you liked having done to you," Sophie said, returning her attention to her breasts and carrying on with sucking, licking, and gently biting them.

"When have I ever told you that?" mumbled Hazel, running her hands through Sophie's hair.

"When you were drunk," Sophie said, laughing. "When else? You're so loose-lipped when you're hammered."

"And you're always horny."

Sophie grinned. "You've noticed?"

Hazel tugged her up to kiss her. "Hard not to. Why do you think we always ended up making out?"

Sophie kissed her harder, smiling against Hazel's lips. Touching Hazel everywhere, she worshipped her toned body and reveled in how good she felt in her hands, wondering if her cunt felt just as good, too. With Hazel's help, she bet she could give her a really nice time, just like Hazel had given her. Her cluelessness couldn't be any worse than when she first tried touching a guy's dick— at least with women, she knew what spots to start with.

Determined, Sophie slid one hand along Hazel's smooth leg, catching Hazel's lip between her teeth. But before she could reach her goal, Hazel rolled them over and started kissing her way down Sophie's tiny body, causing her heart to skip a few beats. Sophie suddenly felt self-conscious for the first time in a very long time. Her body had never been very soft, always more on the bony side—no matter how much she tried to gain weight and fill out her figure. The only part of herself she felt truly proud of was her boobs, which so many people assumed to be fake.

She wondered if Hazel did, too. And if perhaps her body was all hard lines and unpleasant to kiss—something she never wondered before Hazel. Hazel said nothing, though, so hopefully that meant she must have been okay.

When she realized Hazel was heading somewhere in particular, however, she just about yelped and jumped out of her own skin.

"Wait, are you—?"

"Yup. Eating pussy is a favorite hobby of mine. Mind if I indulge in it right now?"

Sophie could only blink, jaw dropping. Hazel watched her closely, those honey eyes flashing as she sank her teeth into Sophie's taut belly. Jesus, she was so damn sexy.

"But you just—I mean, you haven't even cum yet."

"Orgasms aren't always the goal for everyone. Honestly, if we stopped right now, I'd still be happy with what we did."

"I wouldn't," Sophie countered, which earned her a downright cackle from Hazel.

"Don't worry, babe. I'll take care of you," she replied, licking her lips.

Sophie didn't even have the time to think about anything to say in return. Hazel immediately buried her face between Sophie's legs, mouth immediately going for her clit. Sophie's breath caught in her lungs so sharply she almost choked, and she moaned, snatching out to grab fistfuls of the pillow behind her. Hazel chuckled, sending exquisite vibrations that thrummed against her overly sensitive nub. Holy hell, Hazel was a fucking godsend.

Using her lips and tongue in ways Sophie had never experienced from anyone else, Hazel's prowess became transparent when it came to knowing what women liked. Within seconds, she had Sophie thrashing, quivering in the sweaty sheets; crying out in octaves never reached before, climbing heights she never knew existed. Sophie didn't know if her practice came from Hazel's own experience receiving oral or from any feedback she might have gotten after performing it, but she didn't care. Enjoying the ride was all she wanted to do now.

And what a ride it was. Sophie couldn't be sure what Hazel was even doing between her legs, but whatever it was it worked like a motherfucking charm. Every flick of her tongue and strong suck had her shuddering, twisting needily, and begging for more. It was even better when her fingers joined in, delving back into her depths to curl at that spot that drove Sophie wild. She couldn't understand how she ever doubted that women would be better than men when it came to this. Of course they would. Women had to know better than men for most things when it came to sex—except maybe for penis-related tricks.

"Hazel… *Hazel*…" Sophie chanted, wailing her bliss incessantly. "Hazel, oh my God. *Fuck.* I'm gonna cum. I'm gonna cum, baby, I'm gonna—"

Hazel hummed some kind of acknowledging noise and Sophie cried out, pinching her nails so sharply against Hazel's scalp that she was sure it had to hurt. Holding her mouth steady against her cunt, Sophie ground out her waves and moaned with all the wanton lust within her, her world shifting into a blurry mess. Hazel groaned, sending more delightful vibrations through her, but she kept going and helped Sophie ride out the bliss with slower, tender strokes and sucks that prolonged her orgasm beyond what she was used to.

She erupted into bits of laughter when Hazel planted a few last kisses on her inner thighs before removing herself from between them and collapsing beside her, causing Sophie to immediately clasp a hand over her mouth. She hadn't meant to react this way in response to such sensational oral, and it occurred to her how offensive it could be. But then Hazel hauled for a sweet kiss, propping her head against her hand, and Sophie relaxed. Hazel smiled as they pulled away.

"That good?" she asked.

Sophie blinked, mouth parting. She was astounded that Hazel seemed to understand everything going through her head right now. How did she do that?

Sophie's cheeks reddened and she nodded, smiling shyly. "It was just… wow. I think—I mean I always enjoyed it when men went down on me but… I think—

no, I *know* that this was the best oral I've ever had. Who taught you all this?"

Hazel smirked, both pleased and decidedly unsurprised. Jesus. She was so hot. "Mix and match of experiences. My first girlfriend had a lot to do with teaching me what fantastic oral is like, though. She was the queen of it."

"Well, thank you Hazel's first girlfriend," Sophie acknowledged, melting into the bed, completely sated. Her eyes were droopy, still dazed from the strength of her orgasm, her body utterly blissed out. She hesitated before asking, "So… was that all foreplay?"

Hazel snorted then tapped Sophie on the nose playfully. "Nope. That, my lovely Sophie, is what we call lesbian sex."

"Really?" she asked, dubious.

Hazel's eyes crinkled at the corners, lips lifting faintly. "Contrary to popular belief, sex doesn't begin at penetration. Sex is everything before it. From the moment you're having foreplay, you're having sex, honey. Heteronormativity has led people to believe otherwise for most of their life."

"I don't know if I like that way of thinking. If I accepted that, I would have lost my virginity at thirteen instead of fifteen," Sophie mused aloud.

Hazel snickered, tugging her in for another kiss. Sophie responded—at least, she started to before realizing that she'd been the only one who came yet again.

"Wait—don't you want to—?"

Hazel shrugged. "Like I said, it's not everyone's goal to cum. I got more out of this watching you cum twice than I would have if I'd had an orgasm. Plus, I've been fantasizing about going down on you for *so long*. You have no idea how satisfied it makes me to have finally heard you moaning my name and begging me over and over."

"I didn't beg you," Sophie protested, but nagging doubt set in before the words even left her mouth. "Oh shit, did I?"

Hazel preened, looking like the cat that ate the canary. "You can't even remember. God, you have no idea how smug that makes me feel. So worth not having an orgasm."

Sophie smiled. She yanked Hazel close and smoothed her lips over hers, feeling up and down her wonderful dark chestnut-toned body. They kissed like that for a while, spent and blissfully content (at least Sophie was) but full of lazy passion. They cuddled afterward, too full of loving hormones to deprive themselves of the occasion.

It wasn't long before it started hitting Sophie that this might have been a horrible idea. She didn't love Hazel. Well, she *did*, but she wasn't *in love* with her. They were great friends, had been for two years—had they now ruined everything by not talking about what this was going to mean from the start?

She didn't want to date Hazel.

Or anyone, really. She never even wanted to date Zeke, and he was her best friend. They had been best friends *with benefits* for a few years now.

But things weren't messy with him, so maybe there was hope for her friendship with Hazel, too. No two friendships reacted the same way to similar situations, though.

Sophie bit back a sigh. This whole thing was already starting to give her a headache. Or maybe that was simply her hangover coming back into focus now that all the bliss and lust was wearing off. She'd barely noticed it since the moment she and Hazel started seducing each other. Although she wasn't sure she could have so easily forgotten it if she hadn't thrown up beforehand.

Jesus. Had she really just had sex after waking up feeling like such a pile of garbage? The thought was laughable.

Nausea crawled back up her throat. Sophie closed her eyes. Now she wasn't sure if she felt like vomiting because her fragile stomach still wasn't done being angry at her or if it was because this entire friendship was about to crumble into ruins.

A hand swept over her side and the slight curve of her ass, and Sophie shuddered. She chewed her bottom lip. Pushing herself away from Hazel to meet her gaze, Sophie cleared her throat and licked her lips. Hazel blinked back at her, bemused.

"Hey, so um… this might get awkward," Sophie began. "But I think I need to put this out there in case you might be starting to think otherwise right now…" She paused, biting the inside of her cheek. She was tempted to look away, but she kept their gazes locked anyway. A sigh left her mouth. "Okay. Hazel, I think you're really hot and I adore you. You're amazing. But—Well, I don't want to date you. This has kind of… only been a release of sexual tension for me. I don't… feel anything romantic, you know? Like. I'm attracted to you, but I don't—"

Hazel began to crack up and she shook her head. "Sophie, relax. I get you. Know why? Cause' I feel the same. Honestly, if I didn't know you were down with this kind of thing, I probably wouldn't have let you seduce me earlier."

"This kind of thing?" Sophie asked, brows rising. Then she poked Hazel's shoulder. "And hey! We were both seducing each other. In fact, I'd argue that *you* started it. You offered to take my shirt off."

"I was genuinely just trying to help you out. You got yourself all wet."

Sophie scowled. "Yeah right!"

Hazel's grin was edged with mischief. "Okay, maybe I wasn't being totally selfless."

"See! I knew it."

Hazel laughed again and Sophie did, too.

She was so glad that everything turned out okay and that they would remain friends after everything. Friends who fucked and still had the most fun together outside of the bedroom. Who knows, maybe Hazel could even teach her how to give such fantastic oral. Then she could give tips to Zeke—who was the best she'd had when it came to men, but only after some heavy teaching on her part. She didn't realize how much better oral could still be until Hazel.

Sex with a woman was so awesome. In some ways, even better.

Maybe people were actually right. Maybe they really weren't lying when they said lesbians were the best lovers out there.

Women knew what made other women feel good, after all.

Story 6 - Love Me Hard, Love Me Better, Love Me Dirty (Hot Wives, Anal and BDSM)

Bringing a man to bed with her that was not her husband was always an exciting thing. Especially one she'd been eyeing for a while. Alana had spotted Joey at the gym for several weeks now and his stolen looks had not gone unnoticed. How could they—especially coming from such a delectable man?

He was some Chris Evans lookalike type. Light-brown hair, a strong jawline, and not overly bulky, but packing firm muscles, those of which had Alana wanting to lick every single one of them up— particularly the ones on his lower abdomen, pointing like an arrow to his dick.

Naturally, she told her husband about him after a few days of unsubtle glances. Arthur's interest was piqued.

"How old is he?"

"In his early thirties I think?"

Arthur's mouth had lifted. He'd looked back down to his novel, flipping the next page. "You do like robbing the cradle, my love."

She'd smacked his arm playfully. "I'm only forty-seven! That's not exactly a May-December romance. Besides, you're older than me, smart-ass."

"Yes, by two whole months," Arthur had said without looking up, his voice dripping with sarcasm. She'd smacked him again, bringing out the smile he'd been trying to repress. He'd leaned over to kiss her temple fondly. "Bring him over next week when I leave for Vancouver. I'll set up the camera stream."

Alana loved her husband. Loved his openness and his implicit trust. While their marriage had first started off entirely monogamous, Arthur's many travels presented far too many obstacles in their sex life. Arthur was often too tired and jetlagged from his long trips. His stamina was sometimes not up to par, often leaving her hanging. Their phone sex calls were interrupted by business lunches, dinners, and meetings, doing more harm than good.

Alana quickly grew more and more sexually frustrated. She regularly went weeks without sex and fulfilling orgasms, the weight of her unsatisfaction eventually starting to get to her. But when she'd shared the matter with Arthur, instead of being bitter about it or requesting her to be patient like she was sure he would have, Arthur suggested something far more surprising than anything Alana could have imagined: to open up their marriage for her sake, as long as they told each other everything. She could sleep with other men as she liked and get more than her fair share of orgasms, she had been missing in his time away—just as long as she never kept anything from him. He wanted in on the details, wanted to know everything done to her.

Other men probably would have felt jealous. Or maybe even secretly resentful. But Arthur enjoyed her stories—so much so that they made their sex hotter than it already was. Which was saying something considering what kinks they were into.

"You sure your husband is okay with this?" Joey asked as she led him to bed, yanking off his sweaty gym shirt in one fell swoop

"Okay?" Alana's brow lifted. "No, honey. Arthur *loves* this. That camera I told you about in our room? That's not for me. That's so Arthur can watch wherever he is. He loves seeing his wife get fucked by other men. Loves to know how desirable I am. Loves to see me getting all the satisfaction that he can't give me all the time. He's away so often... and he hates to see me left out. Plus, it makes him feel more competitive and like he has to fuck me better than all those other men did... including you." She dragged her hand down his pants and over his cock, feeling him stir from such a simple dose of her attention. "So, be a dear and fuck me like you've never fucked anyone before, won't you?"

"Don't have to tell me twice," Joey said, roughly. He leaned in and kissed Alana hard, hauling off her shirt, too, and cupping her breasts. When he bit on them, Alana leaned back and grasped his hair (lighter than Arthur's salt-and-pepper, but not as thick) and guided his face deeper against her chest.

She thought about what Arthur was doing right now, if he was on the other side of that camera observing them through the stream, or if he was too busy, instead saving the show for later. She hoped for the former. Hoped he was there, gaze unquestionably set on her, lips lifting every time she made sweet, pleased sounds.

The thought alone had her pussy throbbing harder. God, if he was there, she prayed he was taking note of how Joey was touching her. Prayed he was getting himself all worked up, growing ever more competitive. She couldn't wait for him to come back home. To find out how he'd react to some thirty-something man fucking his wife, seeing her handling a cock that wasn't his.

For now, she was with Joey, though. And she'd give him all of the attention that she could. Suck his gorgeous dick like he was *her* king and hope he would be kind enough to return the favor. She always loved oral—especially if she got to sit on their face and ride it.

"Do you want me to be on top?" Joey asked as he slipped off her pants. His brow was furrowed. He was such a good-looking man. Had such nice lips. Such a beautiful fucking body.

Alana caressed his cock through his gym shorts. He was so hard already. "Whatever you want, baby. I just want that magnificent cock inside me."

Joey's eyes flared and his chest rumbled in response. He spread her thighs wide and cupped her cunt, cursing at how wet she was. Alana tipped her head back and reached over her head to take hold of her pillow, exhaling a hot breath. Her lips split into a blissful smile when he broke away from her and kissed down her neck, traversing all the way to the valley of her breasts, past her belly button, and further below.

Alana bit back a sigh, sliding her hand through his thin hair. Goodman. Most of her suitors seemed averse to perform oral on a woman, perhaps because of their lack of skill. But Alana never expected any of them to be wizards of the tongue. She simply enjoyed having a man's mouth down there, even if he didn't know what he was doing. The sight of it was always so sexy, enough to have her cunt running like the river Nile within minutes.

Fortunately for Alana, though, Joey soon proved that he did know what he was doing. Someone had clearly taught him some good tricks, good enough that it had her turning into a panting, writhing mess. What was better, he also seemed to really enjoy it.

"Just like that, baby," Alana gasped, tugging on his hair. "Keep doing that. Right there. I'm gonna cum all over that pretty mouth."

"Would rather you do it around my cock," Joey replied, drawing away from her sopping wet pussy, features dripping with smugness as he crawled up over her form and fitted himself inside her in one solid thrust.

Alana wrapped her legs around his back, locking him inside. Though she was mildly disappointed he hadn't finished her off with his talented mouth, she still closed her eyes and focused on murmuring encouragement and praise into Joey's ear, raking her nails over his skin as he started pounding her into the mattress.

"Say my name. Say my name so your husband knows who's fucking you," Joey grunted, kissing her sloppily.

And say his name Alana did.

It was late Friday that Arthur came back home, dragging his feet through their front door at seven forty-eight just as Alana had settled into the couch to watch one of the playoff matches of her and Arthur's favorite hockey team. She'd barely noticed he was home until the hall light came on. She dropped her popcorn bowl, but managed to catch it before it hit the floor.

"Red Wings are on. Playing against the Rangers tonight," she called.

"Score?"

"Zero to zero. A bunch of shots, though."

Arthur appeared in the living room door frame, in the process of stretching his neck. He smiled when he spotted her, grey eyes gleaming with a mix of fatigue and happiness. He was exhausted, clearly, but overjoyed to finally see his wife again. Alana's eyes softened and she smiled back, offering him the bowl of popcorn.

Arthur dropped his travel bag by the corner and then made his way to her, slumping on the couch and taking the spot directly at her side. His arm immediately opened as she nestled herself against him, plopping the bowl of popcorn in his lap. They murmured a sweet greeting and offered each other a few lingering pecks. Then they settled more comfortably and cuddled, contently.

"How was your night with that gym guy?"

"Joey?" Alana frowned and peered at him, disappointed. "You didn't see the stream?"

"I did," Arthur corrected, kissing her temple. "I just want to hear it all from you."

Alana's cheeks flushed adorably and snuggled him closer. "After dinner? Let's watch the Red Wings kick ass for now."

"You were waiting for me for dinner?"

"Of course. You didn't eat, right?"

Arthur tapped the middle of her forehead, a gentle gesture he reserved for moments of quiet, loving connection. "You know me too well, my love."

Some hours later, when the Red Wings had won and dinner was had, the two of them shuffled into the laundry room to put in another batch, hang the last one, and fold the clothes that were dry. Alana tried to shoo away her tired husband, but Arthur would have none of it and insisted on helping.

"So," he began to say, drowning out the sound of the faint music playing on the radio in the background. "About this Joey."

Alana's lips twitched. "He was a good sport. We had a lot of fun. As you saw," she said, folding the shirt in her hands. She threw him a flirty look, one that she was sure brought a fire to his loins. "What do you want to know? If he gave me better head than you do?"

"I very seriously doubt that," Arthur said dryly. The stare he set on her in return had *her* burning up inside, now. "No, I was thinking more… How you seduced him. How easy was it to get him on board? Did he know about me?" He gave her a lopsided grin, waking one of his dimples, eyes blazing. "Did his dick feel good inside you? So good that your eyes rolled to the back of your head?"

He was self-inserting, there, and Alana knew that. Arthur had never let it slip his mind the one time he made her cum so hard her eyes rolled to the back of her head in the height of her orgasm. She bit the inside of her cheek and took a pair of sweatpants next, folding them neatly.

"You know that's only you," she mumbled, cheeks reddening.

A moment of silence passed, but then Arthur wrapped his arms around her waist, planting a slow, seductive kiss on her neck. "You didn't answer the rest of my questions."

"Oh?" Alana hummed. She closed her eyes and arched her neck to give him space. "Remind me what they were again? I can't remember."

"Bullshit," Arthur growled. "Don't play coy."

Alana giggled, the sound cut off by Arthur shoving down her shirt to kiss and lick her shoulder. "Seducing him was easy. All I had to do was ask him to show me how to work this machine… and he was putty in my hands already. He'd had his eyes on me for weeks, you see… He didn't waste time letting me know what he wanted."

Arthur's hands clawed possessively at her stomach, teeth sinking a little deeper into her skin. Alana closed her eyes but didn't stop him. Wouldn't dream of it. She'd been waiting with bated breath for this ever since he left.

"You're sure you're not too tired to do this, honey?" she asked, biting her lip as he unbuttoned and unzipped her jeans with nimble fingers. She sighed when they slipped past her panties, seizing her heat. She hoped to God he would say he was never too exhausted for this.

"I'm the one asking questions," he reminded her, his tone hot and authoritative as it always became in moments just like these. "And you better start answering them all before I punish you, Alana."

Alana whimpered, hunching over the washing machine when he began to rub her firmly. He parted her legs, causing her pussy to start throbbing, begging to be filled and used already. God, she was so needy. But she knew it would be a while still before he gave her what she wanted most. Arthur was always such a tease, especially when he took the reins. No one would ever guess that her kind, mellow husband dommed his wife behind closed doors, and Alana loved it. Only she ever got to see this side of Arthur, and no matter how many other men she fucked with his blessing, she never gave the gift of her submission to anyone besides him.

"He knew about you. He knew I was married," she gasped, eyes shutting tight as he rubbed her clit in perfect, expert strokes, mouthing messily at the nape of her neck. "He didn't believe me at first when I told him about—our little arrangement. But then I kept insisting. I kept saying he could call you. Or text you. Or see you in person when you came back. And he was so surprised."

His hand pressed more fiercely, rubbing her in vicious circles that had her trembling. She started to widen her thighs, but Arthur smacked her ass smartly and said, "Keep your legs together so I can get these jeans off you. Don't move until I tell you to, and don't speak unless you're spoken to."

Alana held perfectly still, wanting to follow her husband's instructions, to please him—and herself—by yielding. Yet the temptation to disobey was nearly irresistible, because taunting Arthur and flouting his authority in bed (whether an actual bed was involved or not) always led to the most delightful chastisements, those of which Alana could never get enough of.

She fought that impulse, though, like a good sub, and didn't move a muscle until Arthur told her to step out of the pants he'd jerked down to her ankles.

She felt him press a deceptively innocent kiss against her hip. His breath warmed her skin when he said, "There. Now tell me more about Joey."

"It was funny, actually," she went on, picking up the conversation right where they'd left off, as if Arthur hadn't just silenced her. Such a simple order, but Alana knew things wouldn't stay simple for long. She could hardly wait for more. She was too full of lust already, and they had just gotten started. "He almost bailed when I brought him home. Kept asking me if I was sure you were okay with this. If you really knew. If you were really on the other side of that camera, getting off on this." Her breath caught in her throat when Arthur got back up to his feet and dove between her thighs once more, finding her clit with ease. He pinched it. "I think half of him expected you to walk in on us in a rage—"

Arthur huffed a laugh, but he played with her more roughly. "I knew he looked a little hesitant."

"Maybe we should have gotten a better camera," she breathed. "So you could hear everything..."

"Sweetheart, all I need is to hear how loud he makes you moan," Arthur returned.

He flipped her around and manhandled her onto the washing machine. Alana instantly wrapped her legs around him, carnal in her desire. But after one long kiss, Arthur withdrew, separating their bodies completely. He leaned back against the wall and crossed his arms, that air of dominance returning with even more intensity. Alana's heart raced faster.

"Take off your panties and touch yourself."

A shiver ran up Alana's spine. When she hesitated, Arthur's eyes narrowed. "Now, Alana. Don't make me wait. You'll only get punished worse."

It always fascinated her how different Arthur became when sex was in the picture. He was such a loving husband and golden-hearted man, always smiling at everyone and listening quietly. But during sex, a whole new side of him came out. One who loved to worship her even while he was throwing orders at her. It was always there in his eyes. The confidence, the fire. The love.

He was never degrading. Neither of them were much into humiliation, after all. But there was always something in his tone of voice that made Alana feel so desired; so powerful—as ironic as that was. There was an astonishing freedom that could be found in submission, with the right partner. And no partner could ever be better for her than her husband.

Obeying Arthur's command, Alana lifted her hips and slid off her panties, keeping her gaze locked with her husband's. She opened her legs for his view, reveling in the way his eyes dipped to her wet pussy. She ran her hand down with excruciating patience, keeping her lascivious gaze carefully set on him. She played magic on her clit, touching herself in firm, unhurried circular strokes. Arthur wanted a show, and she was going to give it to him.

Arthur's hand curled at his side, but he did nothing. He only said, "Good. Keep playing with yourself. *Slowly.* Keep your eyes on me. Are you ready to answer more of my questions?"

Alana nodded, eager to do as she was told, to be good for him. Arthur's gaze flared hotter.

"How much did you like his cock inside you?"

"I liked it a lot. It was great. Thick… Hot. Reminded me of yours," she replied, a little breathless. "It was *fun*."

"Did you beg for it?"

She bit her lip, shaking her head. "No… No, I didn't."

Arthur frowned and strode forward until he had her caged between his arms. "Now what did I say before I left?"

Cheeks reddening, Alana leaned forward to capture his lips in a fierce kiss, but he evaded her by recoiling away.

"What did I say, Alana?" he repeated, grabbing a fistful of her hair.

He tugged—just sharp enough that it hurt, but not so much that the pain would overcome her pleasure. Her eyes flew shut, a raw, keening sound passing her lips.

Arthur tsk-ed. "And now you've stopped looking at me. You're being extremely disobedient today. How should we handle your punishment?"

Alana opened her eyes again to stare at him pleadingly. She knew it wasn't going to work, though. But she still loved it. "Please… Please, Arthur."

"No," he said, with the ease of a man who thrived on her supplication. "Not yet. Not for a long time."

Alana whimpered. Arthur freed her from his grasp and stepped away, returning to lean against the wall. He stared her down.

"I want you to go upstairs, strip naked, bend over the foot of the bed, close your eyes and spread your legs wide. When you do, I want you to stay like that. And wait for me. You will not touch yourself. You will not open your eyes and glance around to pass time. You will not do anything but stay exactly as you are and think about what I might do to you next."

"How long will you make me wait?" she asked, her voice small and needy.

"However long it pleases me. You don't get to have a say. This is the first part of your punishment."

Alana whined, stroking herself faster. The thought of waiting there for him, spread open for his perusal and sopping wet, was so cruel and torturous in the best ways. She ached for him already. Ached to know what he would do to her when he joined her.

Arthur stepped forward and stilled her hand, forcing it away from her body. His stare was commanding, even as he let her go and brushed some hair from her face. "Upstairs. Now."

Alana scampered off to do just as he'd asked, breaths heavy with desire. She paused at their staircase to glance back at her dom, her husband, and bit the inside of her cheek as she found he had followed, arms casually crossed over his chest. She swallowed and stripped off her shirt, leisurely climbing up the stairs as she dropped the garment over the railing. Her bra was next, leaving her bare as the day she was born and completely at his perusal.

Arthur didn't react, but he didn't take his eyes off her either, his stare only becoming more intense. He was pleased.

"Don't make me repeat myself again, Alana," he called, as she lingered too long, and Alana hurried on with her path.

Her heart was pounding as she followed his instructions. By the time she reached their bedroom, her cunt was so wet it was probably dripping onto the floor. Alana was surprised to find that the most difficult part was keeping her eyes closed. Torturous as the cool air was on her very aroused and wet pussy, accentuating how empty it felt and how much she yearned to have *some* kind of friction, it was the lack of visual stimulation that had her growing antsy more than anything else. Her mind had to fill in on what her eyes could not, haunting her with fantasies and expectations that had her growing even wetter. Had her aching to touch herself and soothe some of her burning desire.

What was Arthur up to as he made her wait? Was he getting ready in the bathroom, stripping naked as well? Was he pounding his cock with thoughts of her, picturing her as she was right now? Was he watching from their camera feed, making sure she obeyed his every direction?

The last thought had her burning up tenfold, the image of this possibility igniting every nerve in her body. She didn't know how she managed not to touch herself. It was all she wanted to do, all she could think about.

Alana had no idea how much time passed before she heard Arthur's voice break the deafening silence of the room at last.

"Good girl. You did exactly what I asked. You can open your eyes, now." When their eyes met, Arthur nodded. "Perfect. Now lie down on the bed and open your legs for me. But keep those hands to yourself, you hear me? I'm not giving you permission to touch yourself yet."

Alana opened her mouth to complain but swallowed her words down as she reminded herself what was at stake, heart racing even faster as she did as he asked. Once she was settled, she chewed the inside of her cheek and waited for his next commands, her pussy aching for him.

Still fully dressed, Arthur merely made his way over to the side of the bed, tracing his finger on one of her peaked nipples. Then he reached into one of their nightstand drawers—the one that kept all their toys and sexual necessities. She whimpered at the realization alone, a sound that instantly drew his attention. His eyes softened and he smiled, brow rising as he started taking out her favorite toys.

"Help me figure out something... Is your good behavior enough to make up for all of your disobedience this week?" he asked, using her hot pink vibrator to trace a path from her breasts to her stomach, going down,

down… Only to stop just at the edge of her pelvis. "Do you feel you should be rewarded right now? I'm tempted to allow you to pick out the toy I'll use for your next part of your punishment…"

He moved the beloved hot pink vibrator away as the last words left his mouth, leaving her so needy that she stamped her foot against the mattress. Bratty and willful, but Alana was beyond caring. She could only imagine what Arthur saw when their gazes met again; she felt so feral that she wouldn't be surprised to learn her eyes conveyed as much.

"Arthur… Arthur please…"

Arthur's eyes crinkled at the corners. He shrugged. "Maybe you shouldn't be rewarded after all. You haven't been obeying any of my orders since I left."

Alana moaned in despair, but her pussy pulsed with even greater veracity and longing, so desperate for some kind of friction that she began rubbing herself on the sheets.

"You'd think that since I left, you haven't been with anyone with the way you're acting…" he murmured, observing her with brazen grey eyes. "Like that guy's cock wasn't enough. Like you didn't get what you needed. And that's not what our little arrangement is supposed to be, my love… You're supposed to be satisfied. Always."

"He was, I swear," Alana said. "It's just… you… You drive me insane."

Arthur's lips curled higher. He reached up and cradled the swell of one breast, tracing the reddened, peaked bud. "You better not be lying to me, sweetheart."

Alana wanted to insist that she wasn't, but Arthur pinched her nipple enough to make her cry out, and she writhed helplessly. He soothed the pain by leaning down and giving her a loving suck, his tongue rolling around the tender nipple in sweet strokes. She caught hold of his hair and Arthur snatched her hand away.

"Hands off," he ordered. "You're at my mercy."

With another man, playing by different rules, that might be frightening, but not with Arthur. Never with Arthur. God, he was so hot when he was like this.

Arthur gave her breast a few last sucks before releasing her. Alana stayed obediently compliant in her silence, staring at him with pleading eyes. Arthur wound his hand in her hair tightly, yanking on it just enough to hurt, exactly as she liked.

"You're being a good girl. Maybe you do deserve to get rewarded tonight. How would you like to get your ass fucked? I know how much you love that."

Alana's breath hitched and her desire flared higher. It took her everything not to frantically nod and start panting like a bitch in heat. It wasn't that Arthur wasn't big on anal sex, but he had to be in a particular mood. And that mood didn't come as often as Alana would like it to. It was a special treat to be rewarded with such an offer—and though she knew her suitors would probably enjoy fucking her ass, she only ever trusted Arthur enough to care for her properly. As much as they flirted with pain play, and as authoritative as he could be, Arthur was first and foremost always most concerned with her pleasure.

There was only one problem, though.

Arthur chuckled. "Look at you. Getting that look in your eyes like there's nothing else you could ever want more. Such a dirty girl. I'll fuck your ass tonight, my dirty girl. I'll fuck it good and hard—"

"Wait—Teletubby, *teletubby*!" Teletubby was their safe word. Nothing could possibly throw off their mood more than bringing up the alienish child show creatures who were the centerpiece of so many parents' nightmares.

Arthur instantly stopped, utmost worry gracing his features. His grip loosened on her hair, turning softer and kind instead. "Are you okay, my love?"

"I'm alright," Alana said softly, warmth flooding her heart. She tucked her hair back. "Arthur, if you're serious about this... I didn't prepare. Would you mind if I slipped in the bathroom and made sure everything is clean and ready?"

Arthur cradled her cheeks between his hands and smiled. "Take all the time you need. And while you're busy, I'll get a couple of ibuprofens for you. I don't plan on going easy tonight, darling... I'll leave you feeling good and raw. Everywhere."

Alana blushed. She nodded meekly and whispered a shy thank you, offering him a sweet peck as he helped her off the bed. She hurried to the bathroom to ensure that everything was as hygienic as could be and in proper shape, unable to stop thinking about what would ensue tonight.

God, how long had it been since they last had anal sex? Arthur hadn't been in the mood for quite a while. They usually reserved this for special occasions, but lately, even this year's special occasions hadn't moved him enough. It couldn't have possibly been a year since their last time, could it?

"Everything okay in there, honey?" Arthur called, just outside the bathroom door.

Alana grinned. "Be out in a minute!"

Arthur chuckled. There was a pause, and then he said—no, *ordered*, "A minute and not a second longer."

Alana pressed her lips together tightly to keep from giggling, practically vibrating from all the excitement.

She fluffed up her hair and finished in the bathroom. When she came out, she blinked in surprise at what she found. Arthur had set up his laptop near the foot of the bed and was waiting by a chair, holding toys and lube that he evidently intended to use.

He smiled when she met his eyes.

"Ready?"

Alana nodded, the anticipation making it hard for her to stay still. She managed, though. Arthur's somber, authoritative stare took over, inducing a shiver from her body. God, he was so fucking hot. She loved her husband.

"Walk over to me," he commanded.

Swallowing, Alana did as he asked, making sure to keep her shoulders straight and her head high. Naked, she stood dutifully in front of him as quiet as a mouse, shyly meeting his gaze. Arthur leisurely ran his eyes over her, his face never revealing anything. He locked their gazes again and stared wordlessly for a short moment, the urge to squirm rushing through her. She refrained, though.

She wanted to ask what the laptop was for, what he had planned for them, but remembered his earlier words.

"I'm the one asking questions."

She knew he wouldn't answer them now, either.

"Bend over the foot of the bed."

Again? Alana thought. Still, she followed his command. She would play along with his game.

She wasn't expecting to come face to face with a paused video—the one their camera had recorded and streamed for Arthur just a few days ago. The one of her and Joey. On the screen, Joey was in the middle of going down on her.

Alana blushed to her roots. She opened her mouth to say something, but Arthur beat her to it.

"You've never actually seen any of them, have you?" he whispered, parting her legs and firmly running up and down the curve of her ass with his hands. He dipped one hand to her cunt, tracing the length of her folds lightly. Once. Twice. Then once more, more firmly. "You've never watched yourself fucking these other men. Seen the way you react to what they do to you. Never seen yourself as you enjoy someone who is not your husband."

His fingers rubbed her clit now, so tenderly it was torture, and Alana squirmed back against him.

"Play it," he said firmly.

Alana did as she was told, but she was more fixated on trying to intensify the pleasure his fingers brought. Arthur was quick to catch on.

"Pay attention to the recording, Alana. Or else I won't fuck your pretty little ass," he warned. He wasn't helping, though, touching her clit harder and working her in ways she liked.

Alana whined, but she obeyed, forcing herself to focus on the home movie playing on the laptop. She quivered seeing Joey going down on her, remembering how good his mouth felt on her pussy. Never better than Arthur, but he was one of the more skilled men she'd had. Some never even wanted to—selfish cowards that they were.

"God, your pussy tastes so good. And you love it so much drenching my mouth. I could stay here for hours, making you cum again and again."

Two fingers slipped inside of her, mimicking the two that Joey had used when Alana was getting closer to her orgasm. Joey's fingers had been slim but rough, calloused from perhaps construction work or maybe musician skills. Arthur's were softer, thicker—having only ever known office work and piano keys. She liked her husband's infinitely better. Liked their thickness, and how Arthur knew exactly where to curl them, exactly what pace she needed most to cum—

"He didn't touch you like this, did he? Did he finger your cunt and hit this spot right here?" He crooked his fingers, rubbing firmly against her g-spot. "I bet he didn't. I bet he tried to go as fast as he could. These young men always think faster is better. But I know you, Alana. I know how you like to be fucked. With my cock, my fingers, my mouth... I know all your places. But he didn't find many of them that night, did he?"

Alana shook her head, moaning and bucking against his fingers. Arthur huffed, pleased. He added another finger, keeping the steady but firm pace just as she liked it for a slow build. Alana grew dizzy.

"I asked you a question, Alana," Arthur ground out.

Alana whimpered. "No..."

Arthur rewarded her with a thumb to her clit, rubbing circles in time with his thrusting fingers. Alana gasped, feeling the knot within her winding tighter.

"Eyes on the screen. Or I'll stop what I'm doing," she heard him warn in her haze. Alana hummed and gathered all of her energy to do as he asked.

"Good girl," he said, moving deeper, reaching all the way within her where she liked most. "Tell me what was going on through your mind right then. He hadn't made you cum when he went down on you, had he? Were you disappointed? Even though his cock was inside you?"

"I… Yes," she admitted, watching herself moaning on the screen as Joey fucked her, maneuvering her legs over his shoulders in order to go deeper. It wasn't long before she was coming, shouting his name as she grabbed his ass, though she remembered feeling slightly off-put by how he'd never gotten her off with his mouth. "I really wanted to cum on that face. You know how much I love to."

"I know how much you love to cum all over *my* face," he corrected, withdrawing his fingers from her needy pussy.

Alana mewled helplessly at the emptiness he left her with. Oh no. Had she said the wrong thing? Had she made him feel less special? He was torturing her and leaving her unattended to punish her, wasn't he? God damn dizzy brain—

The pop of a bottle cap filled the room and Alana's breath hitched, desire flushing her all over again. That was their lube. Most definitely. She'd know that sound anywhere, as pitiful as that was.

A wet, careful finger rubbed around her puckered opening, sending a shiver up Alana's spine. Goosebumps prickled her skin, breaths falling heavier as Arthur rubbed more firmly, quickly arousing the sensitive area. The cap of their lube bottle popped off again and Alana's heart pounded up a storm, anticipation practically shaking her bones.

She could barely register the sound of her and Joey in the recording, especially as Arthur began to play with her opening again, slipping one finger into her ass. The sensation was foreign, but it was one she always welcomed anyway—one that excited her more and more for the promise of what was to come.

As he worked her, Arthur played her clit with his other hand and murmured, "You didn't cum after that, did you? That was your only orgasm. You tried so hard to cum again, but you knew you wouldn't get there before he did. So you faked it, didn't you my love?"

Alana squirmed against his hand, breath catching in her throat. "How—How did you know?"

"Because I know you, sweetheart. I know how you sound when you cum. I know how your face gets all twisted up. I know how you tremble, how your head always tilts back…"

As if on cue, the sound of her heated moan ripped through the room again—only her recorded one. Her faked orgasm. Jesus, had time passed by so fast as Arthur worked her ass? Had Alana really lost herself this much to everything? Or had her time with Joey been shorter than she remembered?

Arthur paused, took his hand away from her clit briefly, then carefully inserted another lubed-up finger, cutting her breath from her lungs. He paused to let her grow accommodated, murmuring a genuine, "Too much?" to which Alana replied with an enthusiastic headshake.

"Sure you don't need more lube?"

Alana smiled dazedly, then ground back against his hand. She reached down to play with her clit. "Not yet…" she reassured him. "I'm okay."

"I didn't tell you that you could touch yourself," Arthur warned, tugging her wrist away with his free hand.

"Arthur…" Alana complained.

"I told you to cum while I was gone. And you didn't listen. Now you don't get to cum until I say so."

"I want you to cum twice while I'm gone. Not by yourself. You'll bring this gym guy over. Let him fuck you so good you can't walk the next day. You'll think of him. Not me. And you'll let him make you cum twice before he does and not any less. You'll be a good girl for me, won't you?"

Alana moaned again, too turned-on by his words. Even if she knew that it meant she would probably have to beg him later, that he was probably going to deny her orgasm again and again, it still rendered her a mess of lust.

God, she missed him. Missed how intense their sex was, how intense Arthur could be. Missed his cock in her mouth, her cunt, her ass—everywhere.

When Alana heard the zipper of his pants come down, her pussy throbbed so fiercely she swore she could feel her heartbeat through it. Arthur's fingers paused, free hand fumbling to no doubt free himself from the confines of his pants. He led himself to her wet, dripping folds, rubbing his cock against them before leisurely slipping inside. Alana was so wet that her pussy offered him no resistance, accepting him as easily as a hot knife through butter. Arthur groaned, unabashed.

"Look at how wet you are. You're drenching my cock... Feels like I'm buried in silk. Is that all for me, Alana? Or did you get wet seeing yourself be unfaithful to your husband?"

Alana shook her head vehemently. "No—For you," she hissed, pushing her ass back against him and gripping the sheets. She blindly reached for the laptop with one hand, shutting it. She didn't think Arthur would mind at this point. "Always for you. No one else can have me wet like this."

Arthur growled, anchoring his free hand against her thigh and setting up a lazy beat. "I bet if I pulled out right now, you'd drip all over the floor." Alana whimpered, locking her ankle behind his to try and keep him from doing so. Arthur chuckled gruffly. "Don't worry, sweetheart. I missed your cunt too much while I was away. Leaving it is the last thing on my mind."

Moaning, Alana quivered around his cock so much she simply had to plunge a hand between her legs and touch herself. She moved in a frenzy on her clit, crying out in protest when Arthur forced her hand away and pounded his cock into her, moving his fingers in tandem with his thrusts with such delicious force that Alana quickly found herself teetering on the edge. She wailed her husband's name with reckless abandon, crying out short, succinct encouragements and trying in vain to meet his thrusts, desperate to topple off that blissful edge—

"Are you going to cum, Alana? Are you going to cum all over this cock like a good girl? Tell me whose cock is pounding into you. Tell me whose name you're going to scream when you cum all over this cock—"

"*Yes.* God, yes. Arthur, Arthur, *Arthur*," Alana chanted, moans growing in octaves with every thrust. She started whimpering as her end became clearer, her arms trembling so much they could hardly hold her up...

And then Arthur stopped. Just like that. Stilled both his fingers and his cock, steadying her with a single, strong hand. Alana's bliss-filled sounds went somber, lamenting the orgasm that was just beyond her reach. She wanted it so much.

"I told you. You don't get to cum until I say so," Arthur said, slipping his fingers out of her to rub circles around her slickened, puckered entrance. Tears of frustration stung her eyes, still reeling from being so close to relief. "You disobeyed me while I was away. Now you need to learn how to follow my commands again."

"I know how," Alana complained, slipping an unsteady hand between her legs. She sobbed in discontentment when Arthur stopped her from reaching her aching destination. "Please, Arthur..."

"You know how?" Arthur echoed, maintaining his grip on her wrist. He slapped her ass hard with his free hand, still slickened with lube, and Alana cried out. "So you chose to ignore my orders?"

Alana buried her face in the sheets, making some noise of denial. Still, she couldn't find her words as Arthur slipped his perfect fingers into her ass again, working them just the way she liked, which had her quivering around his cock and turning into a panting mess once more.

"More?"

"Yes," Alana answered frantically, rocking back against his hand. She needed more than his fingers now. Wanted his cock—but she knew she wasn't ready for that yet.

His fingers withdrew once more, only with the promise of something else to come. It was the most challenging thing for Alana to be patient, having just had her orgasm torn away from her—one which felt like she had been waiting for all week. Even with the great sex she'd had a few days ago, nothing was ever as fulfilling as sex with her husband. Only he could fulfill her true needs— physically and in all other ways.

Something hard pressed against her back end and Alana shivered, biting down on her bottom lip. Arthur rubbed one full cheek tenderly, murmuring, "Ready?"

Alana nodded, taking a deep breath as he started pushing the toy in. It was a butt plug, she was sure—the toy she preferred to use, sleek and all black, just wide enough to make her feel that deep pressure she so loved.

"All good?" Arthur asked, as always most concerned about her pleasure—or at this moment, rather, her level of pain or discomfort.

There *was* some pain but none Alana couldn't handle or didn't like, so she shook her head no, taking the moment Arthur paused to suck another deep breath and exhale slowly, forcing her body to relax. She gasped when the toy was fully settled within, squeezing around it instinctively.

Her head spun and her body throbbed, squeezing around Arthur again and again. She couldn't even hear what he muttered while he ground his hips in a rough circle.

Alana bit the back of her hand, grinding back into him. She only realized he was talking when he growled, "Alana. Pay attention to me. You don't want me to start punishing you again, do you?"

One of his hands inched closer to her ass, a clear warning about what he would do if she did not comply, and Alana snatched out behind herself to touch him anywhere, needing him to know she was all ears for him.

"Good. Turn over and play with yourself while you suck my cock."

Alana shuddered, but she scrambled to do exactly just that, heart beating out of her chest. She reached for him before she even dipped a hand between her legs, licking her lips at the thought of finally having her mouth on him again.

Arthur chuckled but the sound was quickly followed by a groan, mixing the two together. He gently took hold of her hair before harshly tugging down on it, drawing a moan from her that created vibrations against his rock-hard dick. Another groan slipped from his mouth, hand guiding her rhythm vigorously. Alana settled her free hand on his backside, holding it tightly. She squeezed his ass over and over again, every push and press full of need and pure love.

"My dirty girl... you missed my cock, didn't you?" Arthur murmured, tugging on her hair once more. She hummed, pleased. "Missed the taste of me. Makes me want to cum all over your tongue and make you swallow it all. Every. Single. Drop. Spank you for every one you missed."

Alana whimpered, mouth full of him. She rubbed her clit eagerly, sucking him harder, lapping up the pre-cum leaking from his slit. He groaned again, more fiercely, tugging her closer and choking her on his thick girth.

"*Yes.* God, yes," she moaned, words muffled by his cock. She rolled her tongue around his crown like she knew he loved, looking up at him with the most pleading, tempting eyes—or so she hoped. "Please. *Please*. Cum in my mouth, Arthur. I want it. *Please*."

Arthur stared down at her, never once stopping bobbing her mouth over his cock. His intoxicating little grunts and groans persisted, dampening her cunt even more. But he was considering and that gave Alana hope. Hope that he would give in, that he would let himself go and fuck her mouth till her eyes teared up, growling her name as he would cum messily all over her tongue—

"No," Arthur said, removing himself from her mouth so suddenly that she shouted in frustration.

Arthur threw her a warning look and she quieted instantly. She glared back at him, a pout forming at her lips.

Arthur's lips quirked, just barely. "Watch the attitude, Alana."

Alana softened up and swallowed, averting her gaze to convey her submission to her dom. It worked; Arthur let out a pleased huff and kneeled down on the floor, bringing her legs over his shoulders. Alana's heart quickened.

He didn't waste time lunging between her legs and setting his mouth on her wet cunt, cutting the breath from her legs. Alana tilted her head back against the sheets and clung to them with her hands, panting as

Arthur took her clit in his mouth and sucked it rhythmically, just the way he knew she loved it.

With how worked up she was, it didn't take her long to see her end in sight and quickly start approaching it. But Arthur, the tease that he was, never let her reach it— pulling away and denying her orgasm every time it seemed within reach. Punishing her and driving her to madness with a fire of desire and need.

"Arthur, please. Let me come. *Please*," she begged as another orgasm neared. She needed it. So much. So, so much that she thought she might cry if she didn't get it.

But Arthur kept on with his punishment, removing himself from her completely once more. Alana shouted, driven up the wall and desperate, but Arthur rose up and climbed over her in bed to capture her lips in a harsh, demanding kiss.

I'm the boss, it meant. Alana kissed him back, tears pricking her eyes because she was so worked up that it actually hurt. God, it was so easy to forget how much she loved her husband's torture.

Arthur settled himself between her legs. He paused, just for a moment, then tilted her hips up further—until her ass was tantalizingly close to his cock. Alana's heart stuttered, breath hitching then falling heavier with excitement. She bit her lip when he gently started removing the toy, barely managing to hold back her relieved sob when it left her body.

Arthur met her gaze and smiled, if faintly, before his features slipped back into seriousness as he reached for their bottle of lube. He wet his cock very generously with it, coating his fingers again to ensure her ass was still sufficiently slicked up.

He caught her gaze for her silent approval to go on with the next step and whispered, "Don't play tough. Let me know if you think we need more lube, okay?"

Alana meekly nodded. A shiver ran up her spine as the head of his cock tapped her small, puckered hole. She nodded and reached for her husband, whispering back, "As always. Just take it slow, okay? We should be fine."

Arthur rubbed her thighs up and down twice, then seized one of them firmly and used the other to help push his cock inside. He glanced up at her, gauging her reaction, pushing in one tiny inch at a time—always peering back up at her to try and capture any hint that he should stop.

But Alana didn't give him any.

Although she was uncomfortably full and overwhelmed, she felt no inclination to tell him to stop. She liked the sensations—adored them. Felt like she couldn't be any slicker; Arthur had done a good job lubing them up. Maybe had even gone overboard—but going overboard with lube when it came to anal was highly recommended as opposed to not putting enough.

"Okay, my love?" Arthur asked, all traces of authority gone and replaced by his deep, genuine love. He took hold of her other thigh, adjusting his grasp on them so she was more secure against him.

Alana nodded, throwing her arms over her head. She needed more. But they needed to go slow. No matter how much she wanted to beg him to pound her ass until she couldn't even stand upright. Not letting her body accommodate his cock was a sure way to get torn. Or bleed. Or both.

It took a few minutes before he was fully fitted inside. The moment he was, they both moaned in turn, reveling in the moment together. Experiencing different kinds of pleasures. Arthur, likely in heaven because of the tightness of her ass around him. Alana's, though, was more mental—the unbearably full feeling of him, the borderline pain, the intensity of the room. She felt like she could cum already, like she was right there at the wonderful edge and needed just a little something more.

"Fuck. I always forget about how good you feel like this," Arthur muttered, running his hands up her thighs, her sides, then settling over her breasts. He palmed and squeezed them firmly, his eyes full of appreciation. He finally met her gaze.

Alana felt so overwhelmed and full of desire she was sure it was visible. Especially with the way Arthur's eyes softened.

"I'm okay," she reassured him, grabbing one of his hands and squeezing it. "Don't you go mushy on me now. I thought you said you wouldn't take it easy on me tonight."

Arthur's lips quirked briefly and then his eyes darkened. His chest rumbled with a sort of low growl. "You're asking to be tied up talking to me like that," he warned.

Alana grinned and Arthur reached behind him for the pair of handcuffs he'd set aside earlier along with the lube and butt plug, locking them on her wrists tightly. Maybe even a little too tightly.

Still, Alana didn't say anything. Especially not as Arthur pressed the chain link down into the bed, holding it there to lock her in place and restrain her movements.

"Still remember the safe word?"

Alana's stomach quivered, breaths falling choppier from all of the anticipation. "Yes."

"Good. Cause' that's the only word you'll be allowed to say until I'm done with you. That and my name. Nothing else."

Oh, God. Yes. Fuck yes.

Alana's eyes grew wide. Her pussy quivered in need but it would find no reprieve this time. Not in the way it wanted. Her mouth opened to say something—she didn't know what—but she never got the chance to speak.

Arthur started moving, at first slowly—no doubt letting her body grow more accommodated to him. Then, his pace picked up; gentle but fast little pounds that had her gasping and mewling at every turn.

It wasn't long before those turned into firm, punishing thrusts. Alana moaned, barely able to catch her breath between cries of his name. She tried to rise up to kiss him, but he held the chain of her handcuffs firmly down, keeping her just out of reach. Alana complained. Arthur moved more fiercely, bracing himself against his captor hand so he could deliver a hard slap on her ass. Alana cried out, squeezing around his cock as she teetered even closer to her end.

"Arthur," she said, itching so much to touch herself and reach that release. She sobbed, hands clenching in the sheets as she writhed, desperate for more. "Arthur, *please—*"

Arthur clasped his hand over her mouth but didn't relent, pounding into her roughly. His grey eyes lit up like wild embers as he growled, "What did I say? My name, the safe word, and nothing else."

Alana whined against his hand, the words winding the knot in her belly even tighter. She shouted over and over again when he started hammering into her with even more ferocity, intensifying all of the already overwhelming sensations and bringing tears to her eyes. She was so close it was painful. Alana stared up at her husband pleadingly, in the hopes that he would understand how badly she needed him to finally allow her to cum.

How much she couldn't handle another denial, another punishment.

Arthur bent down and kissed her feverishly, bracing himself on the hand holding her to the mattress so he could drop his hand between her legs and rub her clit. She barely lasted a few slow, delicious rubs, going off like a rocket. Breaking away from their kiss, she screamed, unable to think about anything at all, her whole world blurring over in white.

She hadn't even been aware she'd been murmuring until she started coming down from her high. With both hands somehow buried in his hair and holding his face to her neck, soft encouragements and croons of Arthur's name spilled from her mouth as her husband grunted and continued thrusting away.

He came a moment later, groaning into her hair. Alana held him, relishing in the feeling of him grinding and spurting his hot, thick cum inside her ass, a shiver running up her spine. God, she'd missed the sensation so much. While she loved the overwhelming, too-full side of anal, this still had to be her favorite part.

Or maybe this is, Alana thought, as Arthur began to pull out so very carefully, the sensation making her tremble and ache—in the best way. She bit her lip and closed her eyes, holding on to every second, and sighed when he finally left her body vacated.

Arthur chuckled and Alana's eyes blinked open, seeing bliss-dazed grey pools staring down at her. His lips were curled; amused. He lifted her handcuffed hands from around his neck and let them fall onto the bed, bowing to kiss her deeply. She felt him unlock the too-tight restraints, and as soon as her hands were free, Alana cupped his face and kept kissing him, still reeling from the strength of her orgasm.

"Feeling okay, sweetheart?" he asked, gaze full of love and care. He traced her cheekbone and thumbed her chin.

Alana smiled. "Mm. Feeling perfect," she whispered back, raking a hand through his short hair. "I really missed you, Arthur. No matter how many men I have in bed when you're away… I'll always miss you."

Arthur smiled too, his features softened with more than just his post-orgasm bliss. It was love. Plain and simple. Alana knew it. "Because of how good our 'welcome home' sex is?"

A giggle fell from her mouth. She shook her head, considered his question, then shrugged. "Well, partly. I guess." She began to crack up again at the grin that formed on his lips. She traced his jawline, kissing it tenderly. "Because I love you. And nothing and no one can beat the sex we have for that reason alone. No matter how much bigger their dick might be than yours."

Arthur huffed, then kissed her nose. "Oh, how I love your compliments, wife of mine," he teased, eyes crinkling happily at the corners. He captured her lips again, lingering sweetly. "I'll run a bath for you and get you some water?"

"And a snack, please," Alana added with a wry grin, rubbing her sore wrists.

As Arthur got up, she looked around for the ibuprofen he'd gotten for her earlier and heard him call from outside their room, "Pills are on the dresser."

Alana laughed. "I love you!"

"Love you more, sweetheart."

Story 7 - Elevator High (Forbidden Fantasies)

There was that laugh again. The one that tore Violet Reed right out of her focus zone, each and every time. Violet's eyes snapped over in its direction, cheeks warming at the sight of the lean, scruffy-haired man standing over with two of her coworkers a dozen steps away from her. He was grinning, teeth pearly white against his tawny-beige complexion, large black glasses, and navy three-piece suit.

Sebastian Lam; CEO and founder of LEI. He'd been her boss for about two months now, and Violet still couldn't believe she was working for such a hunk. When she'd met him for the first time on her final interview day, she thought he might have been a branch manager of LEI— not the highest-ranking boss of the whole company. She'd assumed that role would have gone to a fifty or sixty-something-year-old businessman, as it typically did. Besides, people didn't usually meet their CEO on one of their entry-level job interviews, either.

But Sebastian Lam proved he was different from the start. He was so committed to his company and its work environment that he wanted to be included in even the little steps. He never let his busy schedule get in the way of getting to know his employees, ensuring they were thriving. His door was always open for those who needed to talk about any work-related issues, yet he still kept clear boundaries conveying that his friendliness and kindness had limits; that there would be consequences to anyone trying to take advantage. He was a kind, charming man, but he took no bullshit. Violet found him too enchanting to watch.

So did all the other ladies in the office, frankly. They all seemed to be crushing on him or fantasizing about the type of sex they could have with him. But how could Violet blame them? She was one of them too, now. Sebastian Lam was the Asian equivalent of a White Knight—the kind of man their Asian grandmothers liked to brag about at get-togethers with friends and estranged family members they only saw once every few Chinese New Year's.

"I'm telling you, if that man was mine, I would never let him out of the bedroom," Jiang, her desk mate, professed matter-of-factly. Her tone had Violet's lips beginning to curl up.

"I don't think you're the only one who thinks that," Violet replied, eyes flickering briefly to some of their other coworkers staring dreamily at their boss. She brushed her sleek black hair over her shoulder and returned to inputting information from a stack of client files on her desk, trying her best to ignore Mr. Lam's wonderful laugh as it rang through the room again.

It was impossible; her gaze still shifted over to him to catch his grin, and Jiang caught her. She grinned. Violet threw her nearest pencil at her, struggling not to laugh as Jiang squeaked in surprise.

Jiang tossed it back. "Of course I'm not the only one! You do, too," she said, sticking her tongue out.

"Do not," Violet lied, throwing the pencil at her again.

Jiang was more prepared this time, though, giggling as she flung it back to Violet. "Do, too!"

"Do not!"

"Liar!"

"I'm not!"

It went on like that, the pencil being tossed back and forth as she and Jiang argued and started cackling together. The two stopped and blushed, however, as their boss's friendly voice sounded across the entire room.

"Having fun, ladies?"

Violet and Jiang ducked their heads shyly. "Sorry Mr. Lam," they chorused, transparently embarrassed, but Mr. Lam simply chuckled and wordlessly brushed them off.

Mr. Lam's gaze lingered on Violet for a split moment, his friendly smile growing as he waved her hello—something which he'd been doing since the first day she started working at LEI. It was platonic; simply something he did to help her to feel welcomed, Violet knew. Still, the gesture had her blush worsening twice-fold, which she hoped he wouldn't be able to notice from where he was as she waved back.

"Lucky bitch," Jiang muttered, urging Violet to shift her attention to her once more.

She found Jiang pouting comically, leaning her cheek into her hand. Violet bit the inside of her cheek to keep from smiling.

"For what?" she asked, going back to her tasks. "Didn't he do that with you, too, when you started? You said he always waves at every new employee for a while."

"For a while," Jiang agreed. "But not *this* long. What did you do? Blow him in the bathroom?"

Violet stiffened, her mouth dropping open. She reddened like a tomato and threw her eraser at Jiang, a garbled sound leaving her. "What?! No way!" she hissed, looking around the room in panic. No one seemed to have noticed her little outburst. Good.

Violet relaxed, swallowed, and ran her hand through her hair. "He's probably just impressed with my work ethic, that's all."

Jiang smiled, sympathetic. "You're right. I'd be surprised if he hadn't noticed all the overtime you do. Probably helps out a lot with our backlog of paperwork."

"Of course he does. He was the first person I asked when I was coming up short on rent, you know? He's really nice. Always makes sure I get the money I need on time."

"Sebastian Lam, the lifesaver," Jiang concurred. "Thank God he exists."

The both of them raised their cups of coffee as if they were vodka shots and cheered to the rare, amazing bosses out there. Then, they went back to work.

She ended up having to work overtime that night again when her little brother Jaxon texted a little before her shift was over that they had forgotten to pay this month's phone bill. Violet groaned, but she powered through and lamented the loss of a hopefully relaxing night. Jiang gave her a sympathetic look and smile, patting her shoulder, and suggesting she take a bath after going home, then bid her goodnight.

Fortunately, Violet's overtime passed quickly. Within three hours, the giant stack of financial papers her manager had provided her before leaving with everyone else had diminished, until nothing but a dozen files remained. Violet briefly considered finishing it, but her growing headache pounded persistently behind her achy eyes, protesting the idea, so she decided against it. She had done enough for the night, she reasoned, sighing as she rubbed her temples. She needed to go home and decompress. Draw herself a bath, maybe—like Jiang had suggested. That sounded so good right now.

Nodding to herself, Violet gathered the remaining files, got up, and dropped them on her manager's desk with a note. She went back and collected her things, stretching her limbs out, stiff from being at her desk for so long. Gosh, the office was so quiet right now; almost eerily so. It was always so odd being here when most of the lights were out and no one else but her was around. Violet was so used to hearing keyboard taps, chatting coworkers, and phones ringing that she never realized how oddly comforting the sounds were until they were gone.

Shaking off the discomfort, Violet headed for the elevator and smiled, thankful to finally be heading home. When the doors opened, she got inside and leaned against the back wall, yawning. She stretched her limbs again, rubbing the back of her neck. The elevator doors closed, but Violet was surprised it started heading up— called by someone else.

Probably the janitor or something, she thought. Though she hadn't seen him clean her floor yet. Had he decided to work his way backward today? Maybe he wanted to switch things up a little.

When the elevator rang and opened its doors again, though, Violet's mouth promptly fell open. Her brown eyes widened, heart pounding up a storm. Because standing right in front of her was Sebastian fucking Lam, the man haunting the wet dreams of every woman working at this building. Including hers.

Mr. Lam was dressed up in a sleek formal gray suit, his hair combed back in a neat hairdo—taming his usually wild locks with class. Her pussy dampened her panties in an instant. Her mouth went dry.

Violet was not the only one surprised.

Blinking out of his momentary jolt, Mr. Lam smiled warmly and made his way inside. He greeted her amicably and Violet's heart stuttered inside her chest, even as he stood a respectable distance away. The elevator doors slid shut and it started heading down, finally.

"Working overtime again tonight?" Mr. Lam asked, his eyes crinkling up at the edges.

Violet stood stone-still, still unable to recover from the suddenness of his appearance. Why was he still here? Why was he all dressed up? Did he not have the chance to go home because he had too many tasks to finish, but still had to attend an event of some sort? Holy shit, he looked so good.

Good enough she wanted to tear his clothes off and beg him to fuck her right here and now.

Shaking off her daze, Violet thankfully brought back her wits before Mr. Lam could suspect anything and she cleared her throat. "Uh—Yeah. I'm—The phone bill—" She clammed up, growing flustered by his sheer gorgeousness. "Oh God, I am *so* sorry," she stammered out, clasping a hand over her mouth. "I didn't know you'd be—I mean, I—"

Words dying on her tongue, her embarrassment barreled into her with enough force to make her dizzy and Violet covered her face with her hands. Jesus, she was such a ditz!

"You're… sorry for being in the elevator?" she heard him ask, clearly confused.

She peeked through her fingers to find him looking at her quizzically, one perfect eyebrow raised. Violet wanted to groan. She just realized how stupid that sounded. How stupid *she* sounded. Why did her boss have to be so damn handsome and dazzling right now? It was screwing with her brain and her ability to think.

"Um… I guess?"

Mr. Lam's black eyes gleamed brighter. His lips curved up with a smile. He chuckled and shook his head, directing his attention to his reflection in the shiny elevator wall so he could readjust his tie. Violet didn't know why it needed adjusting when it already looked perfect.

"I admit I was surprised to see you here, Violet, but I'd never be angry at an employee of mine simply because they happen to share an elevator with me so late at night."

Violet bit her lip, and she hung her head. "Um. Y-Yeah. Sorry. I guess it sounds totally dumb when you put it like that. Sorr—" She cut herself off, cringing. "Jesus. I apologize for apologizing so much, Mr. Lam. That must be really annoying by now…"

Mr. Lam smiled, all friendliness, charm, and warmth as usual. God, he was so nice. So good. It was unfair how much more attractive it always made him.

"It's alright. I've been there, too. Before I started my own company, of course. I remember how it was. I'm the big boss who can fire you for breathing the wrong way, right?"

Violet tucked her hair back, looking away. "Uh… Yeah. Something like that." *And the fact you're stupidly fucking hot and I want you to fuck my brains out right now*, she finished in her head. *I would drop down to my knees and go down on you at the drop of a dime—Oh my God, shut up, brain!*

The damage was done, however. As she looked at Sebastian Lam in all of his gorgeous glory, she couldn't help picturing herself sinking down to her knees right this moment and undoing his pants with greedy hands, Sebastian's thick fingers sinking into her hair as she freed his cock and sucked him for all he was worth.

Her face burned with such intensity she could barely stand to think, the space between her legs growing considerably wetter. Her panties were probably soaked by now. In front of her fucking boss. Jesus Christ. She needed to get herself together—to change subjects *now*. Anything to keep from focusing on her perverse mind.

"Do I look okay?" Mr. Lam asked, prompting her to peer at him. She found him adjusting his tie, still, frowning like he was nervous.

Violet hoped it wasn't to impress anyone else. Not romantically, at least. As far as she knew, Sebastian Lam wasn't married or in a relationship, but who knew? Maybe he secretly had his eye on someone.

The thought made her stomach ripple with possessiveness, brought a fire to her chest. She wanted to sink down on her knees that much more, to prove herself worthy and suck his cock like no one ever had before, to make him *see* her—

Violet mentally shook the thoughts from her head. She had no right to think like that. Mr. Lam was her boss. He could lose his job, ruin his company's reputation. Why would he risk all that for her?

But, God, what she would give for just one night of hot, dirty sex with him. For ten minutes where they'd both be free of any consequences; where he could just pick her up and fuck her whichever way he wanted, ram his cock inside her wet cunt until she screamed—

Fucking *hell*, she needed to get laid. Soon. She couldn't keep thinking like that about her boss.

Swallowing the tight lump in her throat, Violet cleared her throat once more. She ran a hand through her silky black hair. "Um. Yes," she managed to answer at last. She hoped she hadn't been quiet for too long. "Very ha— very dapper, Mr. Lam."

Mr. Lam blinked, glancing away from his reflection in the wall and back at her. He tilted his head, eyes sparkling with transparent amusement.

Shit. Had he caught on to what she'd almost said?

His lips twitched up in a kind smile. "Thank you. I'm supposed to be meeting this big potential partner tonight. I hear he looks down on anyone with poor style. So naturally, I need to look perfect."

You already do, Violet thought. She bit the inside of her cheek to keep from saying so, swallowing the words down. "As I said, Mr. Lam. Very dapper," she repeated. She hoped he didn't notice how her voice got a little hoarser.

Mr. Lam's smile widened. "Thank you, Violet. And please, call me Sebastian outside of work. There's no sense always keeping formalities."

Violet's cheeks reddened again. She wiped her hand on them instinctively, as though that might make her blush disappear. It didn't, obviously. She ducked her head timidly. "Aren't we at work, though?"

Sebastian shrugged, his eyes continuing to sparkle. With one last look at his reflection to check out his hair, this time, he peered back at her and winked.

Violet's heart began to perform a series of dangerous acrobatics and she was rendered speechless, unable to even think. Oh my God. Sebastian Lam was so perfect. It wasn't fair. Violet had never wanted anyone so much.

The elevator dinged and the doors opened again. A confusing mix of relief and disappointment rushed through Violet and neither of them moved to get out. Finally, Sebastian gestured in invitation for her to leave first and bowed a little, though Violet wasn't sure if it was a playful gibe or simply the manners of a well-raised man. Still, she obliged.

When she passed him by, Sebastian said, "Good work, by the way. Mr. Lei told me that your overtime is really making a difference. Come by my office sometime this week and we'll talk about getting you your first raise."

Violet stiffened, freezing in place. Mr. Lam didn't seem to think anything of it, passing her and offering her a bright smile and a chirpy, "Good night. Rest well. You deserve it," and then trotting off to the limousine waiting for him outside. He patted the shoulder of the limousine driver who opened the door for him, then disappeared inside the car.

Violet remained speechless. Her heart pounded. A raise already? How was Sebastian Lam so fucking perfect?

When Violet got home, she first checked on her little brother to make sure he had eaten dinner, cleaned up the empty beer bottles on the living room coffee table by her snoring father, then went upstairs and drew herself a bath—like Jiang suggested.

She hesitated, then decided to light up some candles and throw in a lavender bath bomb. As she waited for her bath to set up, she went to her medicinal cabinet and got some Tiger Balm to soothe her headache. She brushed her teeth and washed her face, then applied the Tiger Balm to her forehead and temples, a relieved hum leaving her lips at the familiar scent. Once that was all done, she undressed, hopped in the bath as it was still filling up, and sighed as the hot water barely immersed her tired muscles but instantly started unwinding her from her long day.

Violet closed her eyes and tilted her head back against the bathtub wall, then started to drift off. Thoughts of Sebastian filled her mind not two breaths later, remembering how amazing he looked tonight, dressed in all of his fancy glory. Her breath caught in her lungs, imagining what unbuttoning his dress shirt from his body might be like. God, if she had her way and life was in her favor more often, how things would have gone differently tonight...

"Working overtime again tonight, Violet?" Mr. Lam asked as he got in, kind and friendly as ever. His smile was respectful, and so was the distance he kept between them—but his eyes, however, roamed her form in a way that was impossible to miss.

Violet's mouth dried and her cunt throbbed. When he noticed she hadn't missed him checking her out, he politely looked away, throat working on a swallow.

Violet bit her lip. "Yes, Mr. Lam. I hope that's okay," she said.

"Nonsense." Mr. Lam replied, forcing a cheeriness into his tone. "Why would it not be? And please, call me Sebastian. We're off the clock. You can treat me like you would treat any other friend."

I don't want to fuck any of my friends, though, Violet thought. Still, she tucked her hair back and said, "Sebastian, then." Violet savored his name on her tongue. It sounded so good. She wanted to moan it all night long, over and over again.

Sebastian's gaze lit up with even more intensity, and Violet blushed. She licked her lips, heart racing and skipping beats as his eyes followed the move. Her stomach churned. "T—Thank you, Sebastian."

Sebastian's eyes were so heated that Violet felt like they were burning her up from the inside. "No problem at all, Violet," he said, enunciating every syllable of her name in a way that made her pussy instantly wet. Her throat bobbed, thighs shifting together as subtly as she could to relieve herself with some friction.

She stopped breathing when Sebastian noticed, eyes dipping down and flaring hotter before looking away. They stood in silence in the elevator, tension so thick not even a diamond hammer could break it. Violet bit her lip again to keep from whimpering, belly twisting in such tight knots it continued to take her breath away. At this rate, he'd have her panting by his hungry stares alone.

Jesus. If he could do that with just a few hot looks and one slow, delicious enunciation of her name, what could he do to her with his cock?

"How do I look—honest opinion. Would you be impressed by this? I'm meeting an important potential partner tonight. Apparently, he's very high on style. Won't waste his time on people with standard fashion."

His eyes flickered her way, still smoky and blistering. Violet nearly shivered, a thrill running up her spine. She swallowed thickly. *How do you look? You look perfect enough that I would cover you up in chocolate and lick every inch of your body,* Violet thought, licking her lips. But she couldn't say that. Not even with the way he was looking at her. She was still his employee. Maybe he was only testing her willpower?

Instead, she settled on saying, "You look incredible, Sebastian. Very handsome."

Violet thought it was respectful enough to be harmless as a compliment. But when Sebastian's stare shot to her once more, her eyes widened and her heart stumbled at the pure heat she found emblazoned in his gorgeous black eyes, inciting her jaw to drop. Violet had never seen anyone look at her like that before—like it was taking all the restraint in them not to pin her to the floor and fuck her senseless. The attraction was undeniable. One look like that from her ex-boyfriends, and they would have never gotten out of bed for days; insatiable with their lust.

Violet's knees shook. She glanced away, fingers beginning to fidget anxiously. Her breaths got choppier, her eyes remained wide. What was going to happen next? Was he going to call her out on the impropriety of the situation, no matter how much he wanted her?

Because he did want her—if at least for that moment. But he was her boss first and foremost, and he could never risk his whole career just because she pushed his buttons. Right?

The elevator doors *dinged*, but neither of them moved to get out. The tension grew higher, higher—until Violet felt like it swallowed all the air between them. When it grew intolerable, Sebastian stepped forward—but not to get out, like her rapidly deflating heart thought. Instead, he stepped towards the panel, pushing the button for his office floor. And then the ones to close the doors.

Violet's heart skipped a beat. Neither of them said anything as the elevator barred their only exit, locking them with their thick tension once more. Sebastian stepped back again, closer to her than he was before. The elevator started going up.

Violet's throat was so dry she barely managed to swallow. "D-Did you forget something, Mr. Lam?" she asked, a little raspily.

Sebastian's gaze snapped over to hers, his black eyes liquid embers of pure desire. Violet's pussy pulsed louder, demanding to be filled.

"Yeah. My head," her boss replied, his voice rougher than sandpaper.

Violet's mouth opened, but she didn't have time to say anything as Sebastian grabbed her waist and whirled her back into the elevator wall, slanting his mouth possessively over hers. Her toes curled in her shoes, a sound of surprise leaving her in a breath, but she was all too quick to respond. She wrapped her arms around his neck, pulling him closer, and moaning softly. Sebastian shoved his knee between her legs, parting them slightly before hiking her up on the wall, drawing a gasp from her. Violet tilted her head back, gaze clouding over as he started rubbing her through her clothes, aiming right for her sweet spot. She whispered encouraging approvals, already riding up the clouds of bliss when none of their clothes were even off.

She barely had the mind to register when the doors of the elevator opened again to his office floor, but thankfully Sebastian did. Not that she really thought she would have minded fucking him in the elevator at this point. He could do whatever he wanted with her. It felt too good to have him like this. Not just because she hadn't gotten laid in a while, but because her attraction to him was also insanely powerful, making her more and more miserable every time she saw his smile, his sparkling eyes. Especially when both were directed at her.

But now she had him.

Sebastian hauled her up around his hips again, and Violet wrapped her legs around him, eliciting a groan from his lips. He carried them both down the hall, stopping a dozen steps away to push her against another wall. His hand plunged between her legs, cradling her wet cunt and hissing something about her being so fucking wet. He rubbed her over her pants, and she began to whine, thrashing and making a mess of his perfectly coiffed hair.

She pulled back and dragged him into a deep kiss, the act squishing his thick, squared glasses against her face. Neither seemed to care, though. Sebastian only kept touching her, rubbing his palm over clothes, creating friction against her clit. Violet rocked against his hand, making pleased sounds and panting.

Good work today, by the way. The words flashed across her mind. Violet's skin prickled. She shuddered, biting down on her lip. *Good girl. You did so good today,* she imagined he said, biting her tongue as she rocked back harder against his hand. *So good I want to bend you over my desk right now. So I could fuck you in front of everyone to show them how much you're my favorite.*

She keened a low cry, scratching her nails against his scalp. She broke away from their kiss harshly tugging on his hair, pulling him back so he would look at her. Sebastian's chest rumbled with a low growl, his eyes hooded with burning want.

"Tell me I'm a good girl," she whispered, so full of need she wouldn't be surprised if she was looking at him pleadingly. "Tell me I did a good job and that I'm your favorite. Tell me—"

Sebastian dove forward and captured her lips in a fierce kiss, breaking away to pull roughly on her bottom lip with his teeth. He grinned. "Praise kink, huh? Don't worry, we'll take care of that, my dirty girl."

Giving her one last harsh kiss full of teeth and tongue, Sebastian wrapped her around him and carried her down the hall some more, soon stepping inside his large office. Violet was sure he was going to carry them both to his desk and start tearing off each other's clothes to carry this thing forward, but instead he walked them both to the end of the room and pressed her into the huge glass window displaying their beautiful city lit up in all its glory.

Violet gasped, taking it all in. She didn't know why that of all things made her think about the event he was missing out on. "Shoot, Mr. Lam—"

"Sebastian," her gorgeous boss corrected with a growl, cutting her off. He lifted her shirt up and pulled her bra down to suck and lick one nipple; already hardened to a peak and rendering her dizzy.

She panted and mewled, tilting her head back against the window. "*Sebastian*. The… The thing you were going to…"

"I'll be late. Who cares," Sebastian replied, snapping off her bra and sinking down to his knees. "No one is on time for these things anyway." He yanked her pants down, and then her panties—with enough force that Violet nearly fell over. Probably would have, too, if it wasn't for his hand holding her steady at her waist.

Her breath hitched as he drew one leg over her shoulder and bit the inside of her thigh, mouth coming closer. "For now, I just want that pretty pussy to cum all over me," he murmured hotly.

His mouth plunged between her legs and drew a cry from her mouth, sucking and licking hungrily like he hadn't eaten in days. Violet grew so light-headed she felt as though she'd lost her mind for a moment, chanting his name like he was her God. She only started coming back to her senses when he undid his pants and freed himself, hiking her up again around his hips. Positioning his cock at her entrance, he slipped inside her slowly and began to rock into her with shallow thrusts. Once he was sure she was good and ready to be fucked, he picked up his pace and rammed his cock deeper, harder.

Soon, his thrusts were so ruthless and good that Violet was shouting time and time again, moaning his name and muttering how good he felt inside her cunt, how much she'd dreamed about this. Sebastian groaned and fucked her with even more fervor, kissing her so sensually she could have come right there.

But then Sebastian lifted her leg carefully over his shoulder, his stare attentive as he watched her face, as though wanting to catch any sign of pain that might tell him to stop. It was a little difficult and stretched out her muscles to the point of discomfort, but Violet didn't let on, too into this to even think about wanting to stop. Her pleasure far outweighed her ache, anyway.

"Fuck. Should have known you'd be flexible," Sebastian murmured. "Such a dirty girl. My good girl. You have no idea how much I've been thinking about this. Thinking about you between my legs, sucking me off on lunch breaks. Thinking about bending you over that desk and fucking your brains out. You're the only one who makes me hard. I've been wanting to feel this pussy around me so badly." He groaned, slowly building up a faster rhythm and grunting his bliss. "Such a good pussy. I love your pussy, Violet. I love how good you feel—"

Violet tightened her good leg around him and snatched both hands to his ass, guiding him in a faster rhythm. She moaned feverishly and smacked one cheek, digging her nails into his skin as her high climbed to heights she never felt before.

"Cum in this pussy then," she breathed, meeting his thrusts frantically. "Fuck me until you fill me up. I've been dreaming about it for so long, please, *please*—"

Sebastian grunted and he flipped her around, trapping both of her hands against the glass and crushing his back to her chest. He moved harder, faster, fucking her like an animal. "Not until you do, sweetheart," he growled.

Violet cried out, reaching between her legs to touch herself. Sebastian's hand got there first, however, and her hand shot out to his hip instead to grab on for dear life. She sang his name over and over, reciting it like it was a mantra. Building pleasure fogged up her mind, at last reaching its breaking point.

Shattering into his arms, Violet let out a breathless cry as white spots danced all over her eyes. Or maybe those were just the blurred-out city lights. Either way, it didn't matter. She didn't care. She just cared about the blissful waves, the blinding, electrifying pleasure coursing through her veins. Nothing else mattered to her— nothing else but the way he panted into her neck, groaning and grunting out his own race to relief. She shuddered and ground against him when he came, banging a fist against the window and letting out a string of curses, his hot sticky wetness spilling inside her in hot spurts.

Breaking from her reverie, Violet bit down the back of her hand and muffled her shout, grinding against her hand. She ground out her high, prolonging the waves with expert strokes as she recalled Sebastian's last words over and over again.

"God you feel so good. Take it all, my good girl. Take all my cum. Take it all in that good, pretty pussy."

When her bliss started waning, a sluggish smile curled her lips. Violet imagined him cradling her in his arms and carrying her to his desk chair, imagined them both slumping into it together and cuddling for hours. Imagined they murmured conversation and loving confessions, free of consequences from the world.

A sigh left her mouth, reality sinking back in. What was she even thinking? Mr. Lam was her boss. This could never happen. Their love would never be permitted, would ruin the image of his business. He probably hadn't even thought about her this way, and here she was exploring a vivid fantasy. This was wrong. So wrong.

At least I got the best orgasm ever out of it, she mused, slumping deeper in the water. *From the ones I've given myself, anyway.*

Would she ever be able to look at him in the eye again without thinking about all the things he said in her fantasy, though?

Shit. That could be a problem, she thought, running her hand through her wet hair. She slung her arm over her eyes, defeated.

...Oh well. You win some, you lose some.

www.ingramcontent.com/pod-product-compliance
Lightning Source LLC
Chambersburg PA
CBHW060610310726
48982CB00003B/511